Praise for the v

The Other Side of Forestlands Lake

Elizabeth (*Gallows Humor*) delivers her signature blend of lesbian romance and murder in this suspenseful outing. Paranormal YA author Willa Dunn steps into her own ghost story when she returns to her childhood summer home at Forestlands Lake. She's hoping to work on her next book and reconnect with her half-sister, rebellious teenager Nicole, but her plans are derailed by a series of spectral visitations. When Nicole gets drunk and almost drowns in the lake, Willa's childhood sweetheart, Lee Chandler, saves her. Lee, now the director of a summer camp for LGBTQ youth, and her daughter, Maggie, join together with Willa and Nicole to investigate the haunting. Between ghostly possessions and cryptic conversations with mysterious neighbors, Willa and Lee rekindle the flame that was barely allowed to flicker back when they were both closeted teens. Though the story hits some speed bumps trying to juggle the tense mystery and the lighthearted romance, the charming characters will draw in readers, and the plot ultimately hangs together nicely. Fans of romantic suspense are sure to be pleased.
-Publishers Weekly

The author uses great descriptions and innocuous little details to give the community surrounding the lake a disturbing personality. This is a nice juxtaposition with the giddiness Willa and Lee feel over being reunited. I enjoyed losing myself in a paranormal story. I'm pretty set in my ways about sticking to the romance genre, but this was a nice change of pace. The book is well paced, and it's spooky enough to raise the hair on the back of your neck without making you need to sleep with the lights on.
-The Lesbian Review

It took only one book by Carolyn Elizabeth for me to decide that she was a must-read author. This is her third and it proves true again. I love Elizabeth's stories but even if I didn't, I'd read her books for the characters. She makes me fall in love with all of them. There are many layers to this book, and so we don't get one mystery but two. Well-thought, complex and thrilling mysteries. Everything came as a surprise yet still made complete sense (in a paranormal way). Carolyn Elizabeth is proving that she could write any genre and I'd want to read it. In this book, you get romance, paranormal and mystery all in one, with each element being as important and as well-crafted.

-*Les Rêveur*

The plot is solid, very interesting and exciting. The pacing is flawless, making the book a page-turner. The protagonists are very likable and I really found myself caring about them. And not only that, I find myself strongly rooting for them to fix things and start a life as it was supposed to be for them. The younger pair of characters are great too, with a very important role in the narrative. The author did a very good job with them, as well as with numerous secondary characters. All in all, a really enjoyable story which I will read again. I highly recommend it, and am looking forward to other books by Carolyn Elizabeth.

-Pin's Reviews, *goodreads*

With every book I've read by Carolyn Elizabeth, I've fallen more in love with her writing, and that continues to be true after reading *The Other Side of Forestlands Lake*. Ms. Elizabeth did a wonderful job with the setting and the eerie mood of this tale. The characters, both main and secondary, are well developed and fit their roles in the story perfectly. Some of the secondary characters really add to the gloomy darkness of the setting. The story itself and the mystery of the tale is intriguing and spine-tingling in all the right places.

I thoroughly enjoyed this paranormal/mystery/romance and have added it to my favorites list.

-Betty H., *NetGalley*

Gallows Humor

At this very moment, my coffee cup is raised in Carolyn Elizabeth's honor because she gave me the perfect blend of an angst-filled, budding romance with endless humor and an enthralling murder mystery that kept me up way past my bedtime. I still can't get over the fact that this story is her debut novel because Carolyn Elizabeth has knocked my fluffy bedroom socks off with her flawless writing and the witty and entertaining dialogue between the characters along with the vivid descriptions of the Jackson City Memorial Hospital and environs.

If you're looking for a story that will keep you on the edge of your seat and have you doubled over with laughter, then this is definitely the story for you!

-*The Lesbian Review*

I always enjoy reading good debuts. It gets me excited to find new authors. I would recommend this book to just about anyone. I think people will enjoy this read. I hope there is a book two because I will be reading it. Almost forgot, I also like the oddball title of the book

.-Lex Kent's Reviews, *goodreads*

Dirt Nap

Yes! This is how you write a sequel, you make it even better than the first. For those readers that were hoping for more of Thayer and Corey, including their relationship, you won't be disappointed. Their connection keeps growing, the chemistry is in your face and every romantic scene is just as good as the most exciting scenes in the book. All the story lines of this book really hit for me. From a little relationship angst to Corey's big problem with a trusted friend, there was always something going on that kept me flipping these pages.

-Lex Kent's Reviews, *goodreads*

This is a perfect sequel to *Gallows Humor* and met all of my... high expectations. Sometimes sequels can be disappointing, but not this one. We have the same mystery, intrigue, and romance that we found in the first book. Corey, Thayer, and all the secondary characters are just as likable and easy to connect with. The romance is still as sweet, and it was fun seeing the two grow together through all the trials they had to endure. It was also fun meeting a few new characters and watching them develop. Ms. Elizabeth not only has the knowledge she needs in pathology and medicine for this story, she also shines in character development. This is what makes both of these books so great.

-Betty H., *NetGalley*

Great second book for Carolyn Elizabeth and a great second in the Curtis & Reynolds series. Just like her debut *Gallows Humor*, this one is also written in third person, from the point of view of both protagonists, Corey and Thayer. The plot is even more interesting, with a very well-done crime/thriller part, and continuation of a really good romance. The chemistry between the two well-defined and likable protagonists is excellent. Add to that a few other very well-written relationships, good pacing, nice ending...and you have a great read.

-Pin's Reviews, *goodreads*

I must admit that this is the second time that I was blown away with this author's captivating writing style. She has really outdone herself with this story because she gave me a riveting romantic thriller that has so many entertaining and laugh-out loud moments embedded within it. This story kept me glued to my Kindle and hungry for more priceless wisecracks from Corey and Thayer. Even though Carolyn Elizabeth did a wonderful job of filling in some of the details and facts from her first book, I would strongly advise you to read *Gallows Humor* before you read this story so that you would get to know more about these lovely characters.

-*The Lesbian Review*

I reiterate from book one, the main characters of Dr. Thayer Reynolds and Corey Curtis are two of the most charismatic characters that I've had the pleasure of reading about in quite a while. Perfect leads in a book that begins in the foulest way, the discovery of a decomposed body. Although the remainder of the book unravels the answers to the mystery via good action and police work, the joy in the story comes from watching Thayer and Corey interact and grow as a couple and as individuals. They show tenderness and vulnerability in small intimate scenes that paint a picture of a couple falling hard and deep. I could easily read another ten of these Curtis & Reynolds books.

-Jules P., *NetGalley*

ZERO CHILL

Other Bella Books by Carolyn Elizabeth

The Other Side of Forestlands Lake

The Curtis and Reynolds Series
Gallows Humor
Dirt Nap

ZERO CHILL

Carolyn Elizabeth

BELLA
B O O K S
2021

Bella Books, Inc.
P.O. Box 10543
Tallahassee, FL 32302

First Bella Books Edition 2021

Editor: Ann Roberts
Cover Designer: Judith Fellows

ISBN: 978-1-64247-198-4

Acknowledgments

This is my pandemic book and I don't know that I'll ever be able to think of it any other way. It's the manuscript I was working on when the first lockdowns hit and life went sideways. Everything was uncertain, exhausting and depressing, and being creative was not the fun escape it should have been. For the first time, writing was work—and not the kind I enjoy. I received the MS back from my editor just in time for the second lockdown to take hold and it seemed a fitting, if painful, way to finish the project.

My family gets first mention this time. It was hard—it still is. Sometimes it was every woman and boy-child for themselves and sometimes we pulled each other along. A lot of times we stayed silent when we should have communicated better and there were times we said things we didn't mean.

We're still here together, we're healthy, we're heavier and will be stronger for having been through this. I love you all very much. Thank you for your continued support of my writing journey and for talking me out of scrapping this entire book when my bad attitude was at its worst.

Thank you to my editor, Ann Roberts, for your encouragement, your patience, and all your words of wisdom. Thank you to the Bella Books family. I very much look forward to seeing you all in person soon.

Peace, love, and vaccines.

CHAPTER ONE

December Twenty-sixth

The Jackson City Memorial Hospital morgue was quiet the day after Christmas and Corey Curtis was hoping it remained so. She wasn't looking forward to a body rolling in for autopsy and harshing on the holiday high she was hoping to hold onto into the new year. The second the thought floated out of her brain the buzzer to the outside door leading to the loading dock sounded and her stomach sank. If she wasn't expecting a funeral home for a pick-up it was going to be a drop-off and a case requiring a post. She enjoyed her job as Autopsy Coordinator, but she had hoped she could hang onto all the good feelings from her lovely and lively first Christmas with her girlfriend, Thayer Reynolds. She wasn't ready to go down the death investigation rabbit hole.

She opened the back door to her friend, Sergeant Jim Collier, and behind him Officer Kelly Warren.

"Merry Christmas, Curtis." Collier held out a tall cup of coffee.

"Ah, just what I wanted." She backed away from the door to let them in along with a blast of cold air. She looked around the loading dock but only saw his car.

"The ambulance got stuck behind a funeral procession, ironically enough." Collier shed is coat and pushed his way into the morgue anteroom, hanging it over the back of Corey's desk chair. "They'll be here in a few minutes."

"I'm in no hurry. Kelly, how'd the rest of your night go?" She raised her brows hoping for some good gossip knowing he gave Thayer's very drunk best friend, Dana Fowler, a ride home.

"None of your business."

"That tells me everything I need to know."

Collier looked between them. "Were you two together last night?"

"At Rachel's Christmas dinner at the coffee shop," she said.

"What? I didn't get invited?"

"You did. Or, at least, Steph did. She said you had plans."

Collier grunted. "She wanted to work the city soup kitchen."

Corey's brows rose. "Wow, man, that's awesome. She is so good for you."

"If you say so," he grumbled, but he couldn't hide the light in his eyes that talking about Steph Austin sparked. She had been his partner for a short time over the summer while they worked the unidentified body linked to a drug trafficking case. The same case that got Thayer assaulted by Harold Crandall and Corey arrested for interfering with the police when she chased after the kids who'd vandalized her best friend Rachel Wiley's coffee shop.

"Who are you bringing me?" Corey asked, leaning against the desk and sipping her coffee.

"Eh, could be interesting. Could be nothing," Collier replied vaguely. "Let's wait for the body and Doc Webster so we can all be on the same page at the same time," he said referring to Corey's boss, the forensic pathologist.

The buzzer sounded and Corey straightened and reached for the phone. "Guess we're about to find out. If you get the door, I'll get Webster."

Corey gloved and gowned before dragging the irregularly-shaped, heavy black bodybag from the ambulance stretcher to the steel table so the paramedics could get back to work.

"Sergeant Collier, I was very much hoping for a quiet week," Dr. Webster muttered as he lumbered into the autopsy suite.

"Don't shoot the messenger," Collier said and snapped open his notebook. "Unidentified, white, adult male found this morning partially obscured by the dumpsters behind the Towne Plaza between the pharmacy and the bowling alley when the trash pick-up came."

Corey winced. "Ah, jeez, I was just there."

"We didn't want to risk any damage with a preliminary search of the body but we saw no obvious signs of trauma or struggle, no blood at the scene, and no weapon of any kind."

Corey unzipped the bag to reveal the body of a young man in dark jeans and dark, hooded sweatshirt, curled up on his side, arms and legs tucked in. "Ooh, boy."

"Frozen?" Dr. Webster asked.

Corey pulled on an arm, the flesh was rock hard and rigid in a way not explained by death and rigor. What skin they could see was bluish and icy. "As if by the hand of the Snow Queen, herself."

Dr. Webster studied the body. "What's your best guess on his weight?"

Corey pursed her lips, considering. "Hard to tell because of his positioning—one-eighty, maybe?"

Dr. Webster stroked his chin. "All right. Nothing for us to do until he thaws. Corey, get his temperature and whatever external you can and pop him in the cooler. Send me an email with the preliminary external exam. Keep an eye on him and let me know when he comes up above freezing."

"How long is that likely to take, Dr. Webster?" Kelly asked.

"Depends on how frozen he is, but from what I can tell just by looking at him, I'm thinking solid. Could be three days or could be as long as a week. If his identity or your investigation turns up something urgent, I can put in a request for CT or X-ray. Don't forget photos."

Corey was already sliding a new card into the camera. "I'm on it. You guys going to stick around?"

Collier nodded. "Give me something to go on, I beg you, Curtis. We're checking through missing persons and we're requesting security footage for all the shops at the Towne Plaza since the last dumpster pick-up, but it would help if we could narrow the time frame or get an I.D."

Corey hooked the stool out from under the autopsy table and stood over the body to start on her pictures. "I can tell you this to start. Based on the position of the body, he most likely wasn't dead *before* he got cold. Pretty classic heat conservation posture or burrowing he's got going on right now."

Getting his clothes off was challenging and the stainless-steel shears crunched through the frosty fabric. With the body so contorted, she had to make multiple cuts and take the clothes off in sections, dropping them into an evidence bag Kelly held out for her while Collier jotted notes about the size and description of every item.

"Check this out." She held up his cut up sweatshirt and indicated the wasp logo. "Looks like he was a Jackson City Black Jacket at some point."

Collier nodded. "Let's pull the high school yearbook photos for the last…" He eyed the body. "How old do you think he is?"

"Hard to say." She looked at his face and nearly naked body. "Seventeen to twenty-five, maybe?"

"That's a lot of photos to go through," Kelly said, apparently aware he was going to be the one slogging through them.

"Let's start with the last three years then. If nothing turns up you can expand from there," Collier said.

Corey got down to his boxer shorts and paused, the sheers hovering over his hip.

"What?"

"Urine stained." She rubbed the thin cotton between her gloved fingers. "Yep."

Collier looked up from his notes. "He pissed himself?"

"Looks like. Could be a response to the decrease in temperature. I just learned this. It's called cold diuresis. Another possible check in the not-dead-before-frozen column."

"You done with that?" Kelly nodded toward the last section of stiff, dark jeans still on the table.

"Oh, yeah." Corey dug her hand in the pockets front and back coming up with only a ragged scrap of paper. "You know I saw a bunch of kids dressed like this at the Towne Plaza the other night," she mused.

"Doing what?" Kelly asked.

"Being dickheads."

"That anything?" Collier gestured to the scrap of paper.

She unfolded it, tilting it back and forth to determine top from bottom. "The fuck?" She held it closer to her face and swallowed hard, her jaw clenching fiercely.

"What now?" Collier asked.

Corey's teeth ground together so hard she could hear them and she backed up, feeling for the counter with a hand, stumbling back against it, her legs trembling.

"Corey?" Kelly's hand shot out and gripped her elbow, steadying her. "What's going on?"

"You got another evidence bag?"

Collier shook a small one open, holding it out, and she smoothed the irregular paper out and dropped it in the bag. He studied the paper through the clear plastic, his eyes snapping up. "This what I think it is?"

She nodded.

Kelly peered at the paper. "I don't get it. Looks like a prescription print out with partial signature and medical license number. Is that the date? That's good. Looks like Christmas Eve he was alive. That narrows things down." He looked up to see Collier and Corey staring at each other. "What?"

"The signature is Thayer's," Corey said.

"Shit."

Collier sighed. "Warren, head up to the ED and ask Dr. Reynolds to join us. I'll call ahead to Manning."

Kelly shot Corey a sympathetic look before disappearing.

Corey sighed and snapped off her gloves so she could run her hands through her hair. "Fuck."

CHAPTER TWO

December Twenty-third

Corey was loose and relaxed after her workout and hot shower at the Women's MMA Warehouse, the gym she frequented. Under doctor's orders, she still wasn't fighting full contact because of her serious head injury six months ago, but it didn't stop her from working on her footwork, throwing punches and honing her technique. She hoped she would soon receive the all clear and return to the ring doing what she loved—getting her ass kicked by Rachel.

She quit toweling off her hair so she could hear what Rachel was saying. "What?"

"This winter sucks, dude." Rachel crammed six small bags of coffee back inside and slammed her locker closed before they had a chance to fall out again.

"Keeps the body count down."

"Yeah?"

"A little, yeah. Extreme heat does, too. No one wants to leave the house if they can help it." Her workload of late had been light.

"Makes sense. I know I don't want to. The roads downtown have been so bad I've been walking the six blocks to the shop at the ass crack. Haven't decided yet which is worse, walking in this cold or driving on these roads."

Corey let her towel drop and hooked her bra. "Least you don't have a half hour drive in this shit."

"You ready to trade in that piece of shit truck of yours yet?"

"You mean vintage?" Corey dragged a shirt over her head. "Thayer doesn't like me to drive it if there's snow forecast, which is pretty much all the time. I have her Range Rover. I'm gonna pick her up at the hospital now."

Rachel snorted and covered it poorly by clearing her throat as she whipped her hooded black peacoat on.

"Just say it." Corey pinned her with a knowing look. She and Thayer, her girlfriend of only six months, had moved in together in the fall. Making the move had felt right at the time, but it all happened incredibly fast and under strange and unfortunate circumstances. It had been an adjustment—for both of them.

Rachel was heading back to the Old Bridge Coffee House, her business, but she paused on her way out and leaned against the door. "As mind-blowingly sexy as Thayer is and as solid as you two are, moving in together was a huge step. And right after everything that happened this summer. Any regrets?"

"What do you think?"

"That's not an answer."

"It's been great—mostly."

"Mostly?"

Corey threw up her hands. "What do you want me to say? There's just...sometimes..."

Rachel's brow furrowed worriedly. "What?"

"I think I'm washing her clothes wrong."

"What?"

"You know like using the wrong settings and shit. I don't even know what all those washer settings really do. And she hasn't said anything. I think she's afraid to hurt my feelings. But she's stopped putting her clothes in the hamper with mine and—"

"Jesus Christ, dude, I thought you were going to tell me you and Thayer were struggling."

"I *am* struggling. With when to use the delicate cycle."

"Read the fucking tag."

"I do. Half of them say 'Hand Wash.' What does that even mean? Is that like soak in the bathroom sink or"—she affected a bad Irish accent— "plunge and scrub, plunge and scrub?"

"What the hell are you talking about?"

"Come on, man, you've never seen *Far and Away*?"

"You're an idiot and I'm leaving." Rachel slung her messenger bag across her chest and called over her shoulder as she pushed through the locker room door, "You guys are coming to Christmas dinner, right?"

"Wouldn't miss it." The locker room fell silent and she reached for her jeans that had fallen to the bottom of the locker.

There was a whisper of movement behind her before a firm hand cupped her ass. "Jesus!" Corey jumped and spun around, crashing against her locker with a wince. "Fuck, Emma! What the hell?"

Emma Leighton, a woman over a decade younger than Corey's thirty-four years, made no effort to hide the crush she had on her. In fact, she often went out of her way to make suggestive comments or to come into physical contact with Corey. It didn't seem to matter to her that they both had a girlfriend. It was a joke to everyone in the gym. Except Corey. She tried hard to be kind in her rejections, but it was getting increasingly difficult.

Emma grinned. "Sorry. Couldn't help myself. Your glutes are tight, girl."

Corey scowled at her and dragged her jeans on. "Didn't know you were still here."

Emma leaned against the lockers uncomfortably close to her. "It's Saturday night. You wanna go get a drink?"

"No thanks." She pulled on socks and jammed her feet into her boots without tying them. "Thayer's expecting me."

"Who?"

Corey sighed heavily. "Go home, Emma." She locked up and hurried out, feeling Emma's eyes on her the whole way.

Dr. Thayer Reynolds pressed against the wall and made herself as small as possible in the entryway of the Emergency Department. She would rather be waiting where it was warmer and talking with Dana, her best friend and head nurse, but if she was spied still hanging around, she would likely get asked to see another patient. She spent the time running through her to-do list in her head. She didn't have to wait long and saw her SUV crunching up the heavily salted, circular drive.

Corey leaned over and flung the passenger door open for her. "Goin' my way, pretty lady?"

Thayer beamed at Corey—a study in confidence with her goofy smile, slouchy beanie, and sexy butch suede and shearling aviator coat. "Always." She hopped in and gave her a lingering kiss, slipping her hand around the back of her head and through her short damp hair.

Corey leaned into the kiss for a long moment before pulling away with a soft sigh. "What was that for?"

"You showered. Good."

"Uh, thank you?"

"Sorry. I was just thinking about the errands I want to run, and if you hadn't showered, you might want to go straight home. The kiss was because I think you're hot."

"In that case, you're welcome. I've got a grocery list actually, so what's on your agenda? I bet we can get it all done with one stop or *efficiency* isn't my middle name."

Thayer stared at her. If she wanted them to eat even remotely healthy and have a meal more advanced than a burger and tater tots, she handled the grocery shopping and most of the cooking when she could and Corey had never protested. "What groceries? I just shopped."

"Never you mind, woman."

"Are you cooking?"

"Just tell me what you need and where."

"Fine. I need the bank, drugstore and post office."

Corey guided the car toward downtown. "We should be able to hit it all at the Towne Plaza, then. It's got the supermarket I actually know my way around. Shouldn't take me long."

"As run down as that plaza is, it is convenient. I'm going to miss it."

Corey's gaze flicked to her. "Why? Where are you going?"

"Not me—it. The Towne Plaza is for sale. I don't know if they're tearing it down or shuffling shops or something else."

"Wait, what? How do you know?"

"Rachel was telling me about it the other day."

"You and Rachel were talking about commercial real estate?"

"We were discussing the city's plans to upgrade the downtown, new loans being offered to small and women-owned businesses, and investment in the arts. The projects this spring will be widening the sidewalks to make the area more pedestrian friendly, new shops and restaurants to bring in the happy hour crowd, and affordable housing to attract graduates from the university to stay—that kind of thing."

"Huh. I didn't know any of that."

"Well, maybe you would if you and Rachel talked about something besides boobs and punching people."

Corey affected a jaw drop. "Is that what you think?"

"Of course not. I'm sure you have scintillating conversations about the latest video games and craft beer."

"I'll have you know we just had a thoughtful discussion on the weather and laundry."

"Riveting, no doubt." Thayer laughed and slipped her hand onto Corey's leg. "Tell me about your day?" She relaxed as Corey talked, letting the anxieties of her day ease with Corey's rambling and often hilarious recounting of even her most gruesome activities. Never in a million years had she thought she would be laughing out loud at a detailed description of how to get more than twelve amputed legs into a biohazard box, but here they were.

Corey pulled her hat down over her ears and turned up her collar against the icy snow blowing horizontally across the parking lot of the Towne Plaza. The early winter had already been brutal with record low temperatures and snowfall. Despite the weather, the strip mall was packed with after-work shoppers and errand runners two days before Christmas.

She jogged to the Range Rover, her overstuffed bags bumping against her legs, and loaded her groceries in the back. One of her surprises for Thayer was making Christmas Eve dinner. She started the car and got out the scraper to clear off the snow and ice that had accumulated in the hour they had been parked.

A piercing wolf-whistle cut through the blustery wind and she looked around for the source. Through breaks in cars crawling past the storefronts she saw a group of four black-clad figures closing in around a woman exiting the drugstore. Thayer.

Thayer was no stranger to unwanted attention and it rarely rattled her. A few months ago she would have skillfully ignored them or told them off, but now she shrank into her coat and kept her head down as they danced in front of her, grabbing their crotches and wagging their tongues.

"Hey!" Corey gripped the long-handled scraper like a club and charged across the parking lot, throwing up a hand to stop the line of cars. The scraper wouldn't do much damage but it might get their attention. She jabbed the nearest kid in the back with the plastic blade. "Back off, asshole!"

Thayer's face was pale and pinched, her lips pressed together thinly as she hurried past Corey toward the car.

"Fuck you, bitch!" The one she poked snarled and spun toward her. They all looked the same, big and bulky in black sweatshirts with the hoods pulled low over their faces and they reeked of alcohol.

A few months ago she may have readied for a fight, but not now. She just wanted to make sure Thayer was okay, get home and get warm. "Unlikely." She flashed them a chilly smile and nodded behind her. "I'm with her."

They went silent for a moment while they puzzled out her words. She turned and stalked back across the road ignoring their slurred taunts.

Thayer huddled in the passenger seat, arms wrapped around herself. Corey turned up the heat and pointed the vents toward her. "You okay, babe?"

"Fine," she said flatly.

"Thayer—"

"I'm fine, Corey. Just drive."

CHAPTER THREE

December Twenty-fourth

Thayer leaned her forehead against the tiles and let the hot water cascade over her for a long time. She had slept poorly and was tense, frustrated, and unable to shake the unease that crept up on her still. She hated it. She would have described herself as self-assured before. Now, she hesitated and questioned everything.

She wiped steam from the small window in the shower. It was one of the few windows that looked out over the front of the house and the twenty-yard, single-lane drive that lead to Old South Road from her house on Rankins Lake. All the other windows, of which there were many, overlooked the lake.

Corey had been out there for an hour already on the overcast Sunday morning. She was muscling the large snowblower up and down the drive, clearing the eight inches of snow that had been dumped overnight.

Corey was unwavering—and patient and understanding. She hadn't pushed for Thayer to talk about what happened last night with those idiots. She had given her space while letting her know she was available if she wanted to talk. She was everything Thayer could ask for in a partner and Thayer was disgusted with herself and her inability to get past her hang-ups.

She shook off her melancholy and finished her shower while mentally scolding herself, as her therapist would have, if she had heard her referring to the effects of her trauma as a "hang-up."

She focused on Corey again for a moment. She could barely see her, even in her bright red parka and snowpants; the blower kicked up so much snow as it fountained off the drive onto the vast white of the property.

Going from a two-bedroom condo owner in the city to an owner of one-and-a-half acres with two hundred feet of waterline had unlocked Corey's previously unrealized outdoorswoman. If Thayer had thought her sexy before, seeing her chainsawing a downed tree, burning a brush pile or pulling up a stump with the mower had her marveling anew at her sheer strength and physicality and practically salivating over Corey's sweaty, dirt-streaked body.

She readied herself for work, her mind occupied with thoughts of their whirlwind romance. Corey had made the move without hesitation, never once uncertain or indicating she didn't feel like it was as much her home as it was Thayer's.

Though Corey had never given any indication that moving in together was something she was hesitant about and willing to commit to fully, Thayer was hyperconscious about not crowding her. She had insisted Corey keep the condo for as long as she wanted. Thayer was the first to admit it came in handy during her late shifts when she was just too exhausted to make the drive home or the weather was particularly bad and the roads were unsafe. There had even been a few occasions where they simply used Corey's condo as their party pad to save their guests from a longer drive out to the lake.

In the end and with her grandmother's blessing, they had done some painting, moved into the master bedroom and redecorated and updated to better suit their tastes. Lil had been supportive and delighted to be involved with the entire process, and the lake house, though still belonging to Lil, felt like the home they were building together—and part of the life they were building together.

Thayer had made it to the kitchen by the time Corey knocked snow off her boots and yanked off her goggles and hat as she opened the front door.

"Jesus, it's cold," she chattered as she kicked out of her boots and pulled off her parka. "And why the hell do you always have to pee as soon as you get outside all bundled up—annoying as hell," she muttered as she raced past Thayer to the bathroom.

"It's called cold diuresis," Thayer said when she returned. "The theory is your vessels constrict to reduce blood flow to the extremities and conserve heat which elevates your blood pressure so your body dumps water to reduce blood volume."

"Didn't really expect an answer to that, but okay."

"Well, you asked. There's a fresh pot of coffee," Thayer said while stalking around the kitchen and great room, eyeing every flat surface and piece of furniture.

"Oh, thank you, that's perfect. What are you looking for?"

"I can't find my damn keys," Thayer huffed, hands on hips, her tension rising again.

"Oh, sorry." Corey poured herself a cup of coffee. "They're in your car. It's warming up."

"You started my car?" Her irritation drained away.

"Yeah. Hope you weren't looking long." Corey jumped when Thayer's arms slipped around her from behind and wrapped beneath her breasts.

"That was very thoughtful," Thayer murmured as she kissed the back of her neck. In low-heeled boots she matched Corey's five foot ten-inch height.

Corey squirmed in her embrace. "Babe, I'm all sweaty."

Thayer nipped behind her ear. "I love you sweaty."

Corey set her mug down and turned in her arms. "Then let's raincheck and we can get sweaty together." She leaned in, teasing Thayer's lips with her own.

Thayer closed her eyes, relaxing into the embrace and returning the kiss for several long delicious moments before sighing deeply and pulling away. "Raincheck to when—next

Christmas? You can be the one to call Nana and let her know we're not coming, then. And since when are you willing to give up a Pond House brunch?"

Corey let her go with a feigned pout. "You're right—I'm not. Maybe after?"

"I'm flattered, really, but you do remember I have a job, right?"

Corey's frown turned genuine. "Who works on Christmas Eve, anyway?"

"Emergency Department physicians. Be grateful I get any time off at all. As a fellow I still get lumped in with the residents—but with top seniority—which is how I'm getting a half-day today and tomorrow off entirely. Once I'm an attending, assuming I'm offered a position, I'm bottom of the food chain again and will have to fight tooth and nail to get Arbor Day off."

"Noted." Corey sipped her coffee.

"Are you going to get a move on and get a shower? We're supposed to be there at nine and if you want to get dropped back off at home before I have to be on shift, we can't dawdle."

"You said 'dawdle.'" Corey chuckled and slurped her coffee until she noticed her pointed glare. "Sorry. Sorry. I'm going. Which ugly sweater do I wear to a festive holiday brunch at a retirement home anyway?"

Thayer rolled her eyes dramatically and poured herself a cup of coffee. "How about the storm trooper cardigan with the red trim?"

"Oh, yeah, that'll look sharp."

It was a gray morning and the white fairy lights decorating the trees along the long drive to the Pond House were still visible, making the snowy, winding drive somewhat fanciful. Corey blinked at the harsh glare of headlights coming right at them as they rounded the corner into the parking lot. "Jesus, buddy." She grumbled at the sleek black car accelerating hard as it edged by them. "Who the hell out here drives a Tesla?"

Thayer craned her neck as the car whipped past. "That's Eric Farmer, I think."

"Who?"

"Nana's financial advisor."

"Huh. Wonder what he was doing out here before nine on Christmas Eve day."

"I wonder, too."

"You gonna ask Lil?"

"None of my business."

"Isn't it?" Corey turned to her as Thayer pulled into a parking space. "You're her POA, healthcare proxy and executor of her estate. Not to mention probably the sole beneficiary."

"Executrix."

"What?"

"Executrix is the feminine form of executor. Like dominatrix." Corey raised her brows. "Hidden depths, Dr. Reynolds."

"In your dreams." Thayer grabbed her purse from the back and opened the door. "We're early but I bet they'll serve us if you're hungry."

"I'm always hungry."

"We don't have a lot of time. Grab the gift, will you?"

"Hold up, babe, it's icy. I've got better boots—take my hand." Corey flung the passenger door closed and her feet immediately shot out from under her at her shift in balance. "Whoa, fuck!" Her arms pinwheeled for a moment before she crashed onto the ground on her side with a whoosh of air. The present Thayer had carefully wrapped went flying under the car.

"Corey?" Thayer's head appeared over her looking far more amused than concerned. "Are you all right?"

"Super. Yup." Corey grunted and propped herself up on her elbow and pushed her yellow-tinted glasses back up on her nose. She still wore them and probably would for the rest of her life. They were essential to protect against the light waves that still occasionally triggered the migraines that started after the head injury she suffered shortly after she and Thayer first met.

The thing she couldn't wear glasses to protect herself from were extreme physical and emotional stress—also guilty of causing one of her debilitating headaches. She hadn't had one in months. She secretly attributed that to the medal she now wore of Saint Teresa of Avila, patron saint of headaches. Her good friend Jim Collier had given it to her as a gift and as an apology after an incident in which his shitty treatment of her was largely the cause of a particularly bad migraine.

Thayer smiled at her clumsiness but refrained from outright laughter and held out her hand. "Maybe *you* better take *my* hand, tough girl."

She collected the present and let Thayer pull her to her feet. "No one saw that, right?"

Thayer brushed snow off Corey's coat. "That's what you're worried about?"

"Well, you know, some of the ladies here think I'm cool."

"Some of the ladies here think you're my *boy*friend," Thayer said as they linked arms and headed up the steps to the front porch.

The great room was warm with a crackling wood fire, and LED candles twinkling amidst fragrant pine boughs mixed with the scent of cooking from the kitchen. The end tables were dotted with plates of cookies and candies and the dining room tables were set festively with doily snowflakes, bells, and clothespin reindeer.

There were other family members already talking with resident loved ones, sharing a cup of coffee before brunch and exchanging gifts. Corey hung up her coat on one of the many hall trees and helped Thayer out of hers. "Don't see her, do you?"

"No. She must be in her room."

"Maybe she was having a Christmas quickie with the Tesla guy."

"What?"

"Eric, whatever."

"I hope not. Eric Farmer is thirty years younger."

"Eh." Corey shrugged. "All the better."

"There she is."

Lillian Thayer was standing in front of an ornate mirror in the hallway applying lipstick and fussing with her hair. "Told you," Corey grinned.

"Knock it off." Thayer swatted her arm and smiled as her grandmother turned toward them. "Merry Christmas, Nana."

"Oh, girls, Merry Christmas." Lillian ambled toward them, her shuffling gait the result of a stroke that had left her partially paralyzed. Her hugs were no less warm for being one-armed and she gave them each a kiss on the cheek. "Our table is ready and we're closest to the fire at my request."

She led them to a table a little apart from the rest and set for three. There was a pot of coffee on the table and a carafe of orange juice. The table was decorated with linen napkins tucked up in wreath napkin rings, and a small ceramic village scene with an LED votive as the centerpiece.

"The place looks lovely, Nana." Thayer held her chair for her and made sure she was settled while Corey filled glasses with coffee and juice. "Did you all help decorate?"

"Those that wanted to, helped, I suppose. Honestly I don't know how much the staff appreciated them bumbling around, tripping themselves up on garland and unwrapping the fake presents beneath the tree." Lillian sipped her coffee.

Corey snorted into her coffee and produced the gift. "Speaking of presents. This is for you." She set the flat rectangular box on the table.

"Is it now?" Lil set her mug down and made a show of rattling the box, eyes flashing merrily.

"Oh, just open it." Thayer smiled.

She lifted the lid and picked up the card atop the folded tissue paper. It was a gift certificate for two to dinner and a movie.

"That's from me," Corey said. "Just let me know when there's something you want to see and I'll come to take you out."

"Oh, how lovely." Lil reached her hand across the table and patted Corey's arm. "For a moment I thought you were suggesting I go on a date."

"Oh, well, you can do that, too. You could take Er—" She jerked when Thayer's foot came down hard over hers under the table. "Never mind." She mumbled and hid behind her coffee mug.

"There's more, Nana." Thayer gestured to the box.

Lillian opened the tissue paper and paused, her breath catching. It was a matted and framed photo taken off the back deck of the house. The sun was low in the sky, lightening after a summer storm, with the arc of a rainbow visible through the clouds and a great blue heron in full flight skimming across the water. "It's beautiful, Jo." Lil referred to her granddaughter by her shortened middle name, Josephine.

"It is, isn't it? I wish I could say it was more than just good timing and a quality phone. We had a larger copy made for the house, too," Thayer said.

Corey hadn't met Thayer yet, but she knew it had been difficult after Lillian's stroke. She had tried to stay at her house which she loved dearly, but it just wasn't safe for her to be on her own. She knew how much Lil missed her property and it was only because Thayer was the one living in it now that she handled giving it up as well as she did.

Lillian swallowed hard several times and ran her fingertips over the glass. "Thank you." She looked up with bright eyes and offered them a wavering smile.

"Oh, Nana, you're going to make me cry." Thayer swiped at her eyes.

"Well, good. I don't want to be the only one." Lil cleared her throat, her smile steadier. "I hope you're not too disappointed, Jo, but your gift isn't ready yet and I'm not sure when it will be so you'll just have to be patient."

Thayer smiled, gently. "That's fine, Nana. I have everything I need."

"I stashed this up here when I was up earlier." Lil produced a gift bag from beneath the table and presented it to Corey.

"For me?" Corey asked gleefully and ripped out the tissue paper and pulled out an orange and yellow, wide-striped knit hat with earflaps and a pompom. "Holy shit. It's Jayne Cobb's hat."

Lil grinned at her. "How did I do?"

"Did you make this?" Corey pulled it down over her head. It was ridiculous and perfect.

"Just for you."

"I didn't know you could knit," Thayer said. "And who is Jane Cobb?"

"The Hero of Canton," Lil and Corey announced together.

"A character from *Firefly*, a television show I like—a man by the way," Corey explained. "I loaned the box set to Lil."

"I can't knit very well but I'm learning and it's a challenge with my limited range of motion since the stroke. I've had a lot of time on my hands this winter."

"Did you watch it all yet?" Corey asked excitedly.

"I still have a few episodes left."

"Which is your favorite so far?"

Any further fangirling was interrupted by the arrival of their food.

CHAPTER FOUR

Corey groaned theatrically and tossed her napkin onto her empty plate. She sat back and resisted the temptation to unbutton her jeans. "That was silly good."

"What, no room for dessert?" Thayer teased. "I hear its cheesecake."

"You don't have to still be hungry to eat dessert. I have perfected the art of eating while full."

"How does that saying go?" Lillian smiled merrily at Corey. "I need someone that looks at me the way Corey looks at food?"

Thayer laughed. "It's true. Sometimes I can't compete."

"Whatever," Corey scoffed. "What about your Tesla man, Lil?" She slammed her mouth closed when she saw Thayer wince.

"I beg your pardon?" Lillian said bewildered, looking between them.

"Corey's just teasing." Thayer cleared her throat. "We saw Eric Farmer leaving when we came in."

Lillian's half smile drooped and she paled so dramatically Thayer leapt to her feet. "Nana!"

"I'm fine. I'm fine." She waved Thayer away. "Sit back down, Jo, before they try and make me take a nap."

"Christ, I thought you were having another stroke," Corey said.

"Nana, what was that about? Why was Eric Farmer here?"

"It's nothing you need to worry about, Jo."

"But it's obviously something you're worried about, so I think you better tell me. Maybe I can help."

"Clearly it's money related and you know my girl is rich," Corey joked, earning a glower from Thayer.

Lillian pressed her lips together into a thin line and didn't comment.

"Nana, please, what's going on?" Thayer asked again.

Lillian appeared to consider her options before answering. "You know as well as anyone what a dive the market took last year. Some of my long-term investments were not as safe as I had hoped and they didn't recover. And the rest of my money is in the house."

Thayer's eyes narrowed, suspiciously. "And?"

Lillian sighed heavily. "You know how expensive it is here."

Corey's jaw dropped. "You can't stay?"

She smiled weakly. "It's not as bad as all that. I have another year before I need to make any decisions."

"What? No. You're not leaving here." Thayer shook her head fiercely. "I'll talk to Eric and I'll make arrangements to adjust my school loan payments so I have—"

"You will do no such thing."

"I'm making the maximum payments. I can defer for a year and still pay off my debt in ten years and when I get a permanent position—"

"Enough, Jo. You work damn hard for your money and I'll not hear of it."

Thayer sucked in a breath at her grandmother's rebuke and looked away, clearly stung.

Corey frowned, shifting in her chair at the unsettling conversation. "What about your mom, babe? Maybe she could—" She bit off her suggestion at the withering glare from Lillian. "Or not."

Thayer sighed. "No, sweetheart, that's not an option."

"What? Why?"

Lil turned glittering eyes to Thayer. "She doesn't know?"

Thayer's eyes slid closed for a moment. "There's nothing to know."

"*She* doesn't know what?" Corey asked. "Your parents moved back to Cuba for your dad's family. Right?"

"Is that what you told her?" Lil eyed Thayer hard.

"It's the truth."

"Yes, but you conveniently left out the part about how they abandoned you."

Corey sucked in a breath and reached for Thayer's hand. "Thayer?"

"It's okay, Corey." Thayer shook her head at her grandmother, her jaw clenched. "Nana, that's *not* what happened."

"Because your father couldn't handle having a gay child and your mother couldn't stand up to him."

"Damn it, Nana, stop it!" Thayer's hand came on the table with a bang, rattling the plates and silencing the room. All that could be heard was the crackling of the fire for a few long moments until Thayer cleared her throat and looked around at the wide-eyed stares. "I'm sorry. It's all right."

"Maybe we should go," Corey said softly into the silence. Her heart hurt at the distance between two of the women she loved more than anything in the world.

Thayer turned to Corey. "I'm sorry. I know I should have been more open with you about my family, but honestly sweetheart, I'm over it. I am. And my relationship with my parents is in a good place. You've been there when we've video chatted. You've met them. We're fine. It was ten years ago and I was already on my way to med school and they already had plans to move out of the country. One thing had nothing to do with the other except in the sense that I thought it would be as good a time as any to tell them I was gay. Yes, my father struggled when I came out, but my mother's support was never in question. She just kept it quiet until my father had some time to process everything. I was not alone. I was an adult. I had friends and I had Nana." She turned to Lil and smiled shakily. "My mother knew I would be well taken care of. I didn't get left behind or cut off or run off the property."

"I'm sorry, babe." Corey smiled gently and squeezed her hand.

"There's no reason to be sorry."

"I'm sure it's easy to be accepting parents from twelve hundred miles away," Lil said.

"The only one still angry about what happened is you."

Lil's eyes flashed in the firelight. "That's what happens when you're disappointed and ashamed of your children."

"Nana, please," Thayer pleaded and reached her other hand across the table to cover her grandmother's weak right hand. "Please, it's long past time to let this go and move on."

"When I finally realized my husband for the bottom feeder he was, I kicked his fat ass to the curb and put my children first. Your mother should have done the same."

Corey's brows shot to her hairline at Lil's harsh words. "Tell us how you really feel, Lil."

Tears glistened in Thayer's eyes, but she didn't let them fall. "Parents are allowed to make mistakes. My father is a good man. You used to think so, too."

Corey's throat tightened at Thayer's sadness and she looked at Lil, imploring her to say something to make this better, but she just crossed her arms and looked away.

Thayer sighed. "Okay, well, we don't need to keep going around in circles about this. We've had this conversation more than enough times before. You know how I feel about it and I know for a fact that Mom has reached out to you. The only one standing in the way of your relationship with your daughter is you, Nana."

Their table fell silent as the server came around. "Are you ladies ready for dessert?" she asked hesitantly.

"Yes, please," Thayer said. "I'm sorry, Nana, this is not how I imagined our Christmas meal was going to go."

Lillian pursed her lips and covered Thayer's hands with her own. "I'm sorry, too, Jo. Let's not talk about this anymore."

"Thank you." Corey grinned as the strawberry cheesecake was set in front of her. "Just to, you know, land the plane about all the financial stuff." She mimed a plane landing on the table with her hand. "Why don't you sell the house, Lil?"

"That's *your* house, now," she said.

"I mean, sell it to *us*," Corey said, forking into her cake.

"What?" Thayer said.

Lillian's expression turned curious as she appeared to consider the possibilities.

"You worked damn hard for what you have, too, Lil, and you deserve to enjoy your..." Corey gestured uncertainly with her fork.

"Dotage?" Lil arched a brow at her.

Corey smirked. "You said it, not me. I have some savings. I have no debt to speak of and my area has really come up in the last few years. After I sell the condo I should be sitting on more than enough cash for twenty percent down for the lake house."

Thayer stared at her. "Corey, that's really generous but—"

Lillian raised her hand. "Hold on. Eric already talked to an appraiser. The house is valued at around three hundred thousand but figures I can list it for closer to three fifty."

Corey shrugged. "Done."

"I hope I don't live so long as to need that much more money."

"Then you can will it back to us."

"Wait. You can't just decide this," Thayer said. "Corey, we should talk about this."

"What's to talk about? We already live there. We don't even need a realtor."

Thayer's brow furrowed and she pinched the bridge of her nose between her fingers. "I can't do this right now. I have to get to work." She stood and moved around the table to pull her grandmother into a hug. "Merry Christmas, Nana. We'll talk about this soon, okay? I don't want you to worry."

"Merry Christmas, Jo." Her grandmother hugged her back, fiercely. "You two enjoy your first Christmas together and don't give me another thought." She winked at Corey over Thayer's shoulder.

"Corey? I can't be late." Thayer was already heading for the door.

Corey grinned at Lillian and leaned across the table to give her a quick kiss on the cheek. "I'll have my people call your people."

Lillian laughed. "You do that, dear. Merry Christmas."

"Thayer, hold up." Corey jammed her new hat on her head and jerked her arms through her coat sleeves as she raced down the steps. She hit the bottom, her feet skidding. She went totally horizontal and landed flat on her back with a painful wheeze. "Shit! What the hell!"

"Corey, Jesus." Thayer hurried back to her looking genuinely concerned this time. "Are you hurt?"

"I fucking give up. Carry me."

Thayer pulled her up and wrapped an arm around her waist for the walk back to the car.

"Do you want to talk about it?" Corey asked when they were back on the road.

"What?"

"There were truth bombs being dropped left and right in there."

"You mean my grandmother telling me she's out of money, may need to move and won't accept my help?"

"For starters."

"Or the other thing?"

"One thing at a time, please." Corey held up a hand. "Lil is stubborn and proud and I don't mean that in a bad way. She doesn't want to be a burden. And she does have money—in the house. It's an easy fix, babe."

"So, she'll accept help from you."

"It's not a loan, Thayer. I'm offering to buy her house where I already live—for free."

"And what about me?"

"What about you?"

"What about my stubborn pride?"

Corey sucked in a long breath. "I see. You still think of it as your house. You don't want me involved."

"That's not it."

"We can put it all in your name. It's not a big deal."

"It *is* a big deal."

"Oh, god, my head hurts." Corey took off her glasses and pinched the bridge of her nose causing Thayer to jerk the wheel as she turned to look at her. "Not like that. I'm fine. Watch the road."

"Don't *do* that."

"Sorry. I haven't had a migraine in so long I wasn't thinking." Corey slipped her glasses back on. "I just want to understand—"

"What my problem is?"

"What your concerns are," Corey finished calmly as Thayer pulled into their driveway.

The muscle in Thayer's jaw worked while she stared out the windshield toward the house. "I just don't want you to feel trapped," she finally said.

Corey was quiet a long time. This had come up before, but not for a while, and she didn't feel they had the time to address it sitting in the car. "What time are you going to be home?"

"I should be back before seven. You want me to pick something up for dinner? I didn't make any plans and I think the Chinese place we like should be open."

"No it's okay. I got dinner tonight," Corey said.

Thayer's brows rose curiously. "Oh, yeah. The groceries."

"Will you give something some thought for me, though?"

"Of course."

"Are you sure it's *me* you're worried is going to feel trapped?" Corey smiled hesitantly. "I mean I know how independent you are and now I get where a lot of that comes from with your parents leaving you and all—"

"Oh, for god's sake, I was twenty-one when my parents moved. I had a wonderful childhood and wanted for nothing. It's not like my parents neglected me and abandoned me at the circus when I was eight years old."

Corey couldn't help a laugh. "Okay, fine. I just want to be clear that I'm all in. So, you know, if there's a hurdle here it's not mine."

Thayer's mouth opened as if to speak, but she remained quiet and turned to look out the windshield again. "Can we talk about this later?"

"Yes." Corey opened the door. "I'll see you soon, babe. I love you."

CHAPTER FIVE

Thayer stood in the nurses' lounge, open tonight and tomorrow to all staff in the ED for the holidays. There were several long tables covered in festive tablecloths with matching napkins, plates and plasticware. There was a perpetually refilled punch bowl and trays of food catered by the cafeteria with additional snacks and sweets brought in by anyone who wanted to contribute. Her own offering of two pans of homemade fudge brownies with caramel swirl, Nana's recipe of course, was down to the crumbs.

There was a constant flow of nurses, doctors, residents, and support staff—porters, environmental services, maintenance and security—in and out all night. Folks were stealing moments to share a meal together, snacking on the run, or piling plates high and covering them with napkins to eat when they got a chance.

Thayer stared, overwhelmed at the options.

"Jesus, I've been eating like a clown car for days and it's not even Christmas yet," Dana said next to her.

Thayer blinked out of her daze and stared at her best friend. She hadn't heard her come in. "Sorry, what?"

"Where were you just now?" Dana perused the offerings. "Everything all right?"

"Do you think I'm afraid of relationship commitment?"

"What? No. Wasn't it your idea for Corey to move in with you? Who said that? I can't imagine Corey."

"No. Nana is having financial trouble and I offered to help, but you know how well she accepts anything she considers charity. Then Corey swooped in and offered to buy her out of the house and she seemed pretty keen."

"Corey has that kind of money?" Dana asked around a mouthful of shrimp cocktail.

"Apparently." Thayer picked at the brownie crumbs and licked her fingers. "Anyway, I got weird about owning a house together, thinking that Corey is going to feel hemmed in, and it's not the first time I've suggested something like that to her. I feel like I'm always going out of my way to make sure she knows she has an out."

"So, what's that about do you think? Has she ever given you any reason to doubt that you're *the one*?"

"No, never. It's not even something we've talked about. We just feel so strong and comfortable and real. It's like we both just knew this was it and nothing more needed to be said."

"So, what's the problem?"

"I don't know. Nothing, I guess." Thayer frowned at the empty pan. "Maybe I'm just borrowing trouble."

"Does this have anything to do with what happened…?"

Thayer winced. "I don't know, maybe. I'm still pretty skittish sometimes, you know, needing to have my back to a wall and be near an exit. Maybe that's what this is."

"It's totally understandable that you feel like that, Thayer. It's only been a few months. You really need to give yourself time to work through everything. Are you still seeing your therapist?"

"Yes, but not as often. I'm okay. Sometimes it just sneaks up on me."

"When you feel cornered."

Thayer blew out a frustrated breath. "That seems to be my pattern when I can't see an escape route, doesn't it?"

"Nothing to be ashamed of, hon, but maybe don't use the 'escape route' analogy with Corey. Kinda brings to mind gnawing off your own hand to get out of the trap." Dana sampled an anonymous puff pastry promptly spitting it out into a napkin. "Ugh, mushrooms."

Thayer laughed. "Thanks, Dana."

"You bet. Anything else?"

"No, I'm fine. Just beat and ready to get out of here. I don't know what made me think it was going to be quiet this afternoon. It's been nonstop sniffles, wrist fractures, fender benders and general drunken idiocy."

Dana stuffed a cheese mini-quiche in her mouth. "Except for the constipated guy."

"Please, don't remind me. Nothing says the holidays like manually disimpacting a grown man."

"Tell me all about it in detail so maybe I'll lose my appetite." She crammed another quiche in her mouth. "When are you done?"

Thayer glanced at the clock. It was five thirty. "Half hour or as soon as Dr. Gregory gets here."

"You rang, Dr. Reynolds?" Watson Gregory III came to stand beside them, rubbing his hands together, gleefully. "Do I have time to eat?"

Thayer couldn't help a smile at his enthusiasm at the buffet despite their still somewhat tenuous relationship. She'd had to confront him within weeks of his beginning with their program for his bullying and harassment. It had been slow and they'd had their setbacks, but their relationship continued to develop both professionally and personally. Now he was on his way to becoming an impressive physician and decent human being.

"Of course," she said. "Far be it from me to deny someone the pleasure of this bountiful feast."

Dana brushed crumbs from her hands and swallowed her mouthful. "You're not eating?"

"I had some earlier. Corey's cooking tonight so I'm going to wait until I get home."

"Uh…" Dana paused, a cracker smothered in cream cheese and salmon in front of her mouth. "Sure you don't want to make a plate to go?"

"I suspect she's been in cahoots with Nana, so no thank you, but I appreciate your concern."

"Your funeral." Dana chomped down on the cracker. "As your last act tonight, and possibly ever with Corey cooking, and on behalf of all of us that still have to work, can you see the kid in two?"

"I can't think of anything I'd like to do more. Want to give me the highlights?"

"Twenty-four-year-old white male who looks shockingly like Adam Rippon, is presenting with fever, fatigue and productive cough of several days. He's fully vaccinated this year and I gave him the good old NP swab," Dana replied. "Vitals and preliminary history are done and I even took the liberty of ordering his chest X-ray, though you'll need to make it official. He should be back from radiology any moment."

"Perfect. You don't even need me," Thayer said, fully appreciating how much nurses contributed to patient care and how impossible her job would be without the exceptional staff the hospital employed.

"Just your signature, really." Dana moved along the buffet when she saw Dr. Gregory blissfully shoveling deviled eggs into his mouth.

Thayer snatched the egg from Dana's hand. "If I don't see either of you again tonight, Merry Christmas."

Her mind was already straying toward dinner and cuddling up with Corey in front of the fire on their first Christmas Eve together and she wrestled her focus back to the present. She moved down the hall toward her last patient while scanning his intake sheet.

Thayer pulled the curtain aside and greeted the good looking, young man with a smile. "Good evening, Mr. Landis. I'm Dr. Reynolds, and I apologize for your wait. It's far busier than I anticipated for Christmas Eve."

"Hello," he replied with a gravelly voice and coughed wetly into a handful of tissues. "You can call me Jeremy." He sat at the edge of the gurney hunkered down in a black hoodie zipped up to his chin, his hands jammed in the front pockets.

"Jeremy, you don't sound like you're feeling very well." She gave him a quick and practiced visual assessment while she snapped on a pair of gloves. His face was pale but for the high color in his cheeks and his eyes bright, signaling a fever. Dana had already taken his temperature, but Thayer touched the back of her hand to his skin, the old-fashioned way. He felt warm even through the gloves. "When did this start?"

"A few days ago, I guess. It's going around. It's nothing serious, I'm sure."

"You're probably right, but we need to be sure you don't have the plague." Thayer pulled the stethoscope from around her neck, happy she could make him smile. "I'm just going to have a listen. It does look cozy but can you unzip your sweatshirt for me for a minute?"

He shrugged out of his hoodie, letting it drop to the bed behind him. "Some of the other guys have been sick, too."

"You live in a dorm?" she asked as she listened to his lungs on both sides, front and back.

"Oh, uh, no, just a group of us in a house," he said followed by a fit of rattling, wet coughing.

She slung her stethoscope back around her neck and palpated his neck, checking for swollen lymph nodes reacting to infection. She pulled a pen light from her breast pocket. "Open." She checked his tongue and the back of his throat. "Any other symptoms? Diarrhea, rash, pink eye, loss of sense of taste or smell?"

"No. Nothing like that," he said. "I'm not gonna have to quarantine, am I?"

"I don't think so, but I'd stick close to home until you're feeling better, and you know, don't go breathing on anyone, wash your hands and wear a mask if you go out." Thayer jiggled the mouse on the desktop in the exam room. "I just want to take a quick peek at your films, but I'm going to put my money on viral bronchitis."

"That's totally what I said but Nora insisted I get checked out and set a good example for the younger guys."

"Nora sounds like a wise woman." Thayer scrolled through the three digital images. "She's like your house mother?"

Jeremy wheezed a laugh. "Totally, but I wouldn't want her to hear you say that. More like a spiritual advisor."

"I could use one of those. Is she accepting new clients?"

Jeremy's lip twitched into a smile, his eyes flashing with amusement. He dug in his back pocket and produced a business card. "Always."

She recognized the rainbow chalice and flame logo in the upper left corner of the Jackson City Unitarian Universalist Church and the name Reverend Nora Warren, Minister. In the upper right of the card was a clever line blend of the letter A and W in the logo for AllWays House. "Walked right into that one, didn't I?"

"You should come by sometime. If nothing else the music is fabulous—when I don't sound like this, anyway—and there's coffee and snacks afterward."

Thayer couldn't help being charmed by him. "Maybe I will."

He cocked his head. "You've probably heard this before but you have an amazing complexion and bone structure."

Thayer laughed. "Thank you, and no. At the risk of sounding vain, my bone structure isn't usually what gets commented on. You may even be the first man to say so."

He laughed with her. "I wasn't hitting on you in case you were worried."

"I never thought you were. But my girlfriend would try to intimidate you just in case." She didn't normally discuss her personal life with patients, but she took a chance and made an exception in this case. She had a feeling Jeremy would appreciate it.

His eyes widened in surprise. "Well, color me pleasantly shocked, Dr. Reynolds." He opened his mouth to speak again but was seized with another fit of racking coughs.

Thayer handed him a couple of clean gauze pads. "Try to clear the mucus and spit into here." She waited patiently while he coughed wetly and wiped his mouth.

"Nasty." He balled up the gauze and looked around for a trash.

Thayer held out her hand. "It's about to get nastier."

He grimaced and dropped the wadded gauze into her hand and watched with fascinated horror while she peeled it open and studied the sticky contents for a brief moment before throwing it away along with her gloves.

"Okay, Jeremy." Thayer went back to the computer. "As much as I've enjoyed chatting with you, and I have, by the way, I have dinner with my girl to get home to and I'm sure you have somewhere to be on Christmas Eve."

"We're doing a big dinner tonight at the house and with any luck I can catch the next bus and be there to carve the turkey."

Thayer printed out a page, signed it with extra flourish knowing it was the last time she had to sign her name for thirty-six hours, before handing it to him. "What you've got going on is viral bronchitis. Very common and will clear up on its own eventually. We can only really treat the symptoms. This is a script for a generic bronchodilator to open your airways and make your coughing more productive to clear all that mucus. Also, you should pick up an over-the-counter expectorant to thin the mucus. Any pharmacist can help you."

He nodded and hopped off the bed, pulling his hoodie on and grabbing his black pea coat off the nearby chair. "The drugstore at the plaza near the church should still be open." He folded the paper into his pocket. "Thanks for taking the time to see me, Dr. Reynolds."

"It was my pleasure, Jeremy." She extended her hand and smiled warmly. "Call me Thayer. I feel like we've shared a moment."

"Good to meet you, Thayer. Merry Christmas."

CHAPTER SIX

Thayer jogged up to the house a few minutes before seven, stamping her feet on the porch to shake the snow off her boots. The house was warm and smelled wonderful. She called as she shrugged out of her coat, "Oh my god, sweetheart, what did you make? I totally knew it. You've been talking to Nana, haven't you?"

She unlaced her boots and kicked them off by the door before heading into the kitchen. "Corey?" She popped open the oven to see the pan of bubbling hot, shepherd's pie. She turned the oven to warm.

In the great room her brows rose with amused interest at the fire ready to be lit and the new floor arrangement—a new faux bearskin rug and an assortment of animal print floor pillows. It wasn't how she would have chosen to decorate, but she appreciated Corey's effort and her intention. "You've been busy. Corey, where are you?"

"Here." Corey stood at the mouth of the hallway, naked but for a towel wrapped around her.

Thayer's lips quirked up into a smile. "Are you coming *from* or going *to* the shower?"

"I was kinda hoping going *to* and coming *in* the shower." She smirked and let the towel drop before heading back down the hall.

Thayer made short work of her blouse buttons while she followed Corey back to the bathroom, picking up the towel on the way and never taking her eyes from Corey's ass.

Corey was already in, and the bathroom steamy, by the time Thayer joined. "Oh, god, what a perfect way to end the day," she sighed as she wrapped her arms around Corey's waist and let the hot water stream over her. She pulled Corey closer and rested her head against her chest, groaning with pleasure when Corey's soapy hands slicked across her back and kneaded her tired muscles.

"How was your day?" Corey asked as she soaped Thayer, up and down, front and back, paying particular attention to her breasts and nipples.

Thayer gasped and squirmed at the delicious sensation. "Not as nice as this." She found her own bar of soap and ran it over Corey's back and ass.

"Well, I should hope not." She traded the soap for Thayer's shampoo and squeezed a mound into her hand.

Thayer scowled at the excessive amount. "What are you doing? That's expensive."

Corey shrugged. "You have a lot of hair." She piled Thayer's wet curls on top of her head and massaged in the shampoo turning her head twice the size with the enormous amount of suds. "Like a Yeti."

Thayer snorted and tipped her head back, eyes closed while Corey massaged her scalp. "If you think you're *coming* in the shower with cracks like that, you've got another thing coming." She opened an eye long enough to get her bearings and smacked Corey on the ass.

Corey yelped. "Didn't even hurt. I've recently been told my glutes are tight."

Thayer's eyes popped open. "By whom?"

"Oh, uh, just…It was nothing…"

"Never mind." She moved Corey out of the way so she could rinse her hair. "I can guess."

"Fuck," Corey muttered and began lathering her own hair. "Did I just ruin the moment?"

"You mean, did mentioning an inappropriate comment made to you by a woman who is *not* your girlfriend, but wishes she were, ruin your chance at getting laid?"

Corey's mouth turned down and hands dropped to her sides leaving her short hair, thick with suds sticking out in every direction. "Is that a rhetorical question?"

Thayer tried to pretend she was grumpy, but she couldn't pull it off. She didn't have a single care for the silly girl from the gym. Right now, Corey was at her most adorable—sexy, soapy, and just like the rest of her, her glutes *were* tight. She gripped Corey by the hands and turned her back under the shower spray, running her hands through her hair to get the suds clear.

Thayer's hands trailed down Corey's neck and rested on her shoulders before she stretched up the couple of inches she needed to meet Corey's lips in a wet, teasing kiss.

"Mmm." Corey hummed her appreciation, wrapping her arms around Thayer's waist and pulling them together tightly as she deepened the kiss.

Thayer could feel Corey's abdomen flexing against her and knowing how much Corey wanted her, aroused her faster than any touch. She slid her hands between them, cupping her small perfect breasts, hardening her nipples to points with a flick of her thumbs.

Corey groaned her approval; her head tilting down to kiss and nip along Thayer's neck. Her hands slid down, one over her ass and one between her legs.

Thayer gasped when Corey's fingers pressed against her. She widened her stance, her mouth dropping open when Corey's fingers slid inside her and she sucked in a breath. "I thought you were the one coming."

Corey buried her face in Thayer's neck, her teeth finding purchase against her shoulder as she held her up with a grip on her ass and her hand deep inside her. "You first," she murmured.

Thayer clung tightly to Corey's shoulders, her head dropping back as the heat of her building arousal washed over her. Her belly clenched and her legs weakened, driving her onto Corey's hand. "Oh, god."

"I've got you." Corey said, her left arm tightening around Thayer's waist and the fingers of her right hand stroking her inner walls.

"Don't let go." Thayer breathed as the ball of sensation inside her coiled and grew with every curl of Corey's fingers. Whatever she was doing was building her orgasm painfully slow. It was exquisite and nearly intolerable.

Thayer's hips bucked against her hand and her fingers dug into the water-softened skin of Corey's back—no doubt leaving marks. She panted, her head dropping against Corey's shoulder. "What are you...doing to me?"

Corey's own breathing was labored. Her only answer was to sink her teeth into Thayer's shoulder. She only had a moment to think on the pain of it before her entire body tightened and she clenched around Corey's hand. "Oh, that's it." She shuddered and gasped, her orgasm overtaking her with wracking explosions of sensation.

The cooling water felt wonderful against her overheated skin as she came down. Corey slipped out of her, but Thayer was grateful for Corey's hands still on her waist. Her head dropped against Corey's chest and she caught her breath, feeling strength return to her lower body. "Wow. What did I do to deserve that?"

Corey wrapped her arms around her back and held her close. "It's better to give than to receive, right?"

"While I won't argue the sentiment, I feel like invoking scripture is ill-timed at the moment."

"Scripture?" Corey turned off the water.

"What you just said, 'better to give than to receive,' is from the Bible." Thayer accepted the towel Corey handed her.

"No, it isn't. It's like a Christmas saying or something."

"From the Bible." Thayer wrapped the towel around her head. "Acts."

"Who?"

"Never mind." She laughed and wrapped her arms around Corey's waist, pulling her in for another kiss. "You are a wonderful and generous lover and I love you very much and I am very, very hungry."

"I've got a plan for that."

"Ugh. Don't invoke Liz either. I'm still mad as hell we don't have a woman president."

"As you wish. Let's eat."

Corey's Christmas Eve dinner was consumed with enthusiasm on the bearskin rug in front of the fire while dressed in their best loungewear. Corey moved her empty plate to the coffee table and topped up her wine glass. The fire crackled merrily and filled the otherwise dark room with just enough light to see Thayer's beautiful auburn hair and bronze skin.

"So, how did I do on dinner?" she asked, eying Thayer from behind her wine glass.

Thayer mopped her last bite of biscuit around her empty plate before popping it into her mouth. "Passable," she mumbled around the mouthful, her twinkling eyes giving away her delight at the meal she didn't have to prepare.

"I'll take it." Corey fiddled with her glass. "You ready to talk about what was bothering you earlier?"

"You really want to spend Christmas Eve talking about my lingering anxieties and misplaced control issues?"

"Is that what it is? Is your hesitation about buying the house about everything that happened this summer?"

"Yes, I think so. I'm working through it."

"You know I'm right there with you, babe. I think about it, too. We've been through some shit. I mean, everything is really great, but was choosing to move in together before we had our feet back under us really the right thing to do? I totally get it if you need to take a step back and—"

"I don't. I appreciate your use of the word 'we' but I'm not so fragile. You can put this on me. I know the issues are mine, but you don't have to worry about me. I'm okay and I want this. I want all of you and all of us, whatever that brings—including home ownership."

"You'll let me know if something bothers you?"

"I always do."

"You know what I mean."

"What you've offered to do for Nana is so incredibly generous. I just wish I could take care of you like that."

"Are you serious? It's only money, babe. And you've literally saved my life."

"I don't know about that."

"I do. Besides, I know what ED docs' salaries start at and that'll be you in six months. At which time I will expect to be a kept woman. You can then lavish me with gifts befitting The Real Lakehouse Wives of Jackson City."

Thayer laughed, her eyes alight with mischief as she crept like a jungle cat across the rug, holding Corey's gaze with her own. "How about I lavish you with gifts right now?"

Corey's eyes flashed and desire clenched her belly. She quickly set her wineglass out of the way before Thayer crawled up her body and straddled her lap, whipping Corey's shirt over her head and pushing her shoulders back to the floor. "I humbly accept your gifts," Corey said breathlessly.

Thayer descended on her like a woman starving, her tongue and teeth finding Corey's most sensitive skin with every nip and suck. Corey groaned and writhed under the onslaught, her hands gripping Thayer's shoulders as Thayer made her way across her torso, over her breasts and down her sides.

Corey gasped and trembled when Thayer kissed her way across her belly and dropped down between her legs, sliding her pants off. Without another word she nudged Corey's thighs apart and closed her mouth over her.

Corey sucked in a sharp breath, her body turning to jelly when Thayer's tongue darted out, flicking and circling and driving her wild with need. "Oh shit, babe," she sighed, her hips rocking with the tempo Thayer set. "I'm so close…"

Corey stopped breathing, her back arching off the floor when her orgasm roared through her. Thayer's mouth licked and sucked her until she collapsed back with deep shuddering groan. "Holy shit…"

CHAPTER SEVEN

December Twenty-fifth

Corey woke as she often did with Thayer tickling the skin of her right arm as she gently traced the images of her full-sleeve tattoo—the sultry mermaid and three dolphins swimming overhead in the sun dappled shallows of the vibrant seascape.

She eased her arm around Thayer and pulled her in for a kiss, closing her mouth over hers and teasing her lips open with her tongue, deepening the kiss and smiling around Thayer's sigh of pleasure. "Merry Christmas, babe," Corey murmured when she finally pulled away.

"Merry Christmas, sweetheart." Thayer beamed at her, golden eyes flashing. "I have a gift for you before you get out of bed."

"Mmm, again?" Corey tucked her hands behind her head. "I suppose."

"Not that kind of gift." Thayer pulled a box from beneath the bed, presenting her with an expertly wrapped flat box in blue and silver paper with silver ribbon and two tiny silver bells.

"Ooh, fancy." Corey sat up excitedly.

Thayer watched as Corey picked carefully at the paper, careful not to tear it. "Why can't you take this much care with my clothes?"

"Oh, shit, I knew that was coming. It's just so pretty. Did you wrap this yourself?"

"I did and don't change the subject."

Corey lifted the lid, brushed aside the tissue paper and cracked up. She held up the bright green, long-sleeve pajama top with elf collar and green and red striped bottoms. "Sweet."

She jumped out of bed and pulled the pajamas on, mischief on her mind when she turned around to model the outfit. As goofy-looking as it was, it showed off her body. She saw the clear desire in Thayer's eyes and smoldered back at her while she ran her hands suggestively down her chest and abdomen. "I do love me some waffle knit."

"May I feel?" Thayer asked hopefully.

"No, you may not." She bounded over to the bureau, pulling a similarly sized flat box from the bottom drawer and bringing it back to the bed.

Thayer eyed the box wrapped in red and green paper with *Star Wars* characters wearing Santa hats before tearing the paper apart and ripping open the box. "Oh, I see," she said dryly.

"What? Great minds, right?"

Thayer held up a gray and red, V-neck, jersey nightshirt with two images of festive green tree ornaments right over the chest. "It looks very…fitted."

"Well, try it on and we'll see."

Thayer shimmied into it without getting out of bed and wriggled her hips to slide the dress down over her legs beneath the covers.

"Well?"

Thayer threw the covers off and stood on the bed, letting the garment fall naturally just below her knees. It even had a slit up to her thigh, and as expected, the ornaments sat perfectly over her breasts with the neckline showing an indecent amount of cleavage.

"Looks cozy," Corey deadpanned. "It's long-sleeve."

Thayer mirrored Corey's move and slid her hands up her sides and over her breasts, slowly. "It is very soft."

"Is it?" Corey moved back onto the bed onto her knees, sliding her hands up Thayer's legs and over her ass to grip around her waist. She kissed her through the material, and pressed her face against her belly. "So, it is."

Thayer's hands threaded through Corey's hair while she lowered herself to her knees and Corey's arms circled around her back, pulling them together. "I do believe this gift is more for you than for me."

"What could ever make you think such a thing?" Corey kissed along Thayer's neck, across her collarbone and down the exposed skin of her chest.

Thayer wrapped her hands around the back of Corey's neck and dropped her head back to give Corey's exploring mouth better access. "Just a hunch."

Corey held her close and cupped each ornamented breast, eliciting a soft gasp of pleasure from Thayer. "I believe there's something in it for you, too."

"Show me," Thayer murmured before closing her mouth over Corey's and toppling them onto the bed.

Corey, dressed again in her elf jammies, popped the cork and poured them each a generous glass of prosecco. She splashed in orange juice and dropped in a handful of raspberries while Thayer, in her very sexy nightshirt, cooked omelets and bacon.

"Come on." Thayer nodded toward the great room, her hands full with plates. "Bring my drink, please—and the bottle."

Thayer, a plate in each hand, smoothly lowered herself cross-legged onto the bearskin rug. The forks didn't even rattle. She settled in front of the crackling fire Corey had already started.

"Now you're just showing off." Corey pursed her lips and eyed the two partially full glasses in one hand and the bottle in her other, debating whether she was going to try and duplicate the move Thayer did so effortlessly.

"Don't do it," Thayer said smugly. "It's harder than it looks and you'll spill my drink—or hurt yourself."

Corey snorted, narrowing her eyes, but heeded her warning in the end, handing over Thayer's drink and setting the bottle on the coffee table before sitting across from Thayer on the rug and accepting her plate of food.

They ate for several minutes before Thayer set her half-finished plate on the table and went to the tree to retrieve another impeccably wrapped, rectangular box and brought it over to Corey.

She admired the intricate crisscrossing red ribbon over silver paper. "Hidden depths, Dr. Reynolds."

"I gift wrapped at the mall over the holidays for a couple of years in high school."

Corey fought outright laughter when Thayer sighed dramatically, as she delicately unwrapped the paper without tearing it.

"Now you're just doing it to irritate me."

Corey winked at her and lifted the lid. "Hey, very cool." Her eyes lit up as she flipped through the items—an entire new wardrobe of workout clothes with various superhero logos including full Wonder Woman sports bra, shirt and compression shorts. "Thanks, babe."

Thayer lounged against some pillows and sipped her drink. "I expect a fashion show montage set to music later."

"I bet." Corey set the box aside before heading to the tree to retrieve another present in an *Avengers* gift bag adorned with festive snowflakes.

Thayer accepted it. "It's heavy." She pulled out the tissue paper to reveal three books. "What's all this?"

"Sadly, I don't make the time to read for pleasure that I once did, at least not anything longer than a comic book. These are copies of a few of my favorites I wanted to share with you."

"Most of my reading as an adult has been textbooks and journals. *Stranger in a Strange Land* and *Where the Red Fern Grows* I know of, but *The Deed of Paksenarrion*, I've never heard of."

"It's one of the only books I've read more than once. Paks is my hero."

"Huh," Thayer mused. "Science fiction, high fantasy, and a children's book about a boy and his dogs. You have surprisingly eclectic taste in reading."

"Yeah, I don't know, maybe." Corey considered that for a moment. "If you read them I think you'll find they all share similar underlying themes of faith, perseverance, and living your truth. Why are you looking at me like that?"

"I guess I was just thinking about how much we still have to learn about each other." She stacked the books in her lap and leaned forward on her hands to give Corey the sweetest kiss. "Of course, I'll read them. They're meaningful to you."

Corey grinned, never doubting that Thayer would fully understand the importance of what she was sharing with her.

Thayer checked her watch. "I have something else for you, but it's not time yet."

"Okay." Corey filled their glasses with the last of the prosecco. "I will try and contain my curiosity, and in the meantime watch you open your last gift from me."

"Every day with you is a gift."

"Are you drunk?"

"Getting festively day buzzed. Do we have another bottle?"

"Yes. Keep in mind we still have Rachel's orphan Christmas party. Dinner is at five." Corey brought back a large, white, square box, unwrapped but for a giant red bow on the top. She set it on the floor in front of her. "Don't open it until I get back."

CHAPTER EIGHT

Corey topped off drinks again. "You know it's not even noon."

"That's what afternoon naps on bearskin rugs are for." Thayer eyed her mischievously over her glass. "I sincerely doubt Rachel is going to care if I show up tipsy to her party."

"I think it's a requirement, actually." She crossed her legs and gestured to the box. "Okay, open it."

Thayer set her glass down and flung off the lid. "Oh, are we having a beach theme party in winter?" She placed on a wide-brimmed sun hat and new tortoiseshell sunglasses. Beneath that were a pair of pink flipflops, a bottle of sunscreen and small bottle of tequila.

"Something like that." Corey grinned excitedly as Thayer continued to uncover items in the box.

She arched a brow as she held up a sexy and simple black bikini. "Another gift for you, I see. Is everyone going to be dressed like this?"

"Probably." Corey worked very hard to not picture Thayer in that bikini while she smoothed lotion over her back.

Thayer pulled out more tissue and looked curiously at a thick letter-size envelope. She glanced at Corey before she unfolded the stack of papers. Her brow furrowed as she looked at a picture of a tall, grinning, older couple holding coconut cocktails with little umbrellas and a sign that read, *Merry Christmas! We can't wait to meet you, Thayer!* "Why are your parents in my Christmas gift?"

"Keep reading."

Her hand went to her chest. "Oh, my god, Corey—an itinerary? You bought us tickets to Key West?"

"Merry Christmas, babe." Corey's smile faltered after a moment. "It's okay, right? I mean, after what you told me about your folks I don't want this to be weird."

"It's more than okay." Thayer's golden eyes flashed brightly and she smiled adoringly at her. "When do we leave?"

"The fifth."

Her face fell. "Of January? Are you crazy? My schedule is set months in advance. I can't even—"

"Don't worry, I took care of all that."

"What the hell does that mean? Did you get me fired?"

"No, come on," Corey laughed hesitantly. It had all seemed like a good idea at the time and she had been all puffed up at her cleverness. Now that it was happening, she was beginning to worry that it was going to come across as really sneaky and controlling—just the kind of behavior Thayer would not appreciate. "I checked your schedule and picked your lightest week and found someone to pick up two shifts for you."

"Someone, who? Please, tell me you did not intimidate Watson into taking my shifts so we could go on vacation?"

"I did no such thing. I merely asked him and he was happy to help me out."

"I'll bet. And what do I owe him?"

"Nothing. In exchange, I scored him two very-hard-to-come-by reserved seating tickets to Rachel's December charity concert with the Byrne Trio a couple of weeks ago. He was out to impress a young lass who is, apparently, a big fan of the bodhran and fiddle. I also got him into her New Year's party to hobnob with the city's elite."

Thayer's expression softened. "That's it?"

"That's it," Corey replied, relieved at the small upturn of Thayer's lips and the brightening excitement in her eyes. She proudly held out her arms. "Now, will you come over here and give me the thanks I deserve?"

Thayer flung the box from her lap and launched herself at Corey, wrapping her arms around her neck and peppering her face with kisses.

Corey rocked back with Thayer in her arms, searching out her lips in an excited teeth-crashing kiss. "So, we're happy now?"

"We are ecstatic now. And highly aroused by your initiative and resourcefulness—and well-made drinks." She shifted forward, pressing Corey down onto the rug while kissing along her neck.

Corey caressed Thayer's hips and grinned up at her when Thayer straddled her. "Is this my last present?"

"No, but we have time for an extra."

Corey gasped as Thayer's hands slid up beneath her shirt and cupped her breasts, rolling palms over her nipples and sending a sharp streak of desire straight between her legs. "I don't think you're going to need that much time."

Thayer shifted down on her, raising Corey's shirt higher and lowering her mouth to her breasts while sliding a hand beneath the waistband of her pants and between her legs. "I guess not," she commented, her fingers tickling through the wetness.

Corey sucked in a sharp breath, hips jerking against Thayer's touch. "Oh, babe." She groaned, feeling her walls contract strongly around Thayer's fingers. Her arousal built unstoppably fast. Thayer's fingers curled and pumped, driving her toward orgasm without hesitation. Her belly clenched and her insides fluttered with her impending release.

Thayer circled her clit with her thumb in a pulsing rhythm for only a few minutes before Corey arched hard and climaxed with a long groan. "Oh, fuck," she breathed and dropped back against the rug. "I'm so fucking easy."

"I have no complaints, sweetheart." She brushed hair out of Corey's eyes and kissed her slowly. She pulled away at the sound of a text message on her phone. "Now, we're out of time."

When Thayer jumped up to check her phone, Corey propped herself up on her elbows. "I feel used."

Thayer replied to the text while pulling the last large box from beneath the tree. "Open this one now."

"Uh, okay." Corey straightened her clothes and tore the paper off the box to reveal the picture of the silver and blue, all terrain snowshoes with matching poles. "Holy shit."

"You like?" Thayer glanced up from her phone with a smile.

"I love." Corey was reading the specs on the outside of the box. "These will be so great to go around some of those trails around the lake—or across the lake. You got some, too, right?"

"No. I'm not much of a winter sports person."

"Well, who am I going to snowshoe with?"

Thayer shrugged dismissively. "Right now, I need you to find something to do somewhere else for twenty minutes or so."

"What? Why?"

"Now, please."

Corey heard the door opening and closing several times while she was in the shower and getting dressed. She was trying to take her time to give Thayer her space for whatever she had planned, but her curiosity was driving her mad. She dressed in thermals, intending to take her snowshoes out for a spin. She had to work off some of the holiday food she had already overindulged in, especially if she wanted to gorge again tonight at Rachel's party.

She figured a half hour was long enough as she listened at the bedroom door for any activity. Hearing nothing, she walked slowly down the hall. "Is it okay to come out now?"

She got no response and didn't see Thayer in the kitchen. She headed around to the great room and stopped in front of the fireplace, her jaw dropping at the sight. There was a gangly, brown puppy rolling on its back, legs in the air, on the bearskin rug in front of the fire. "You're not Thayer. Or, are you?"

The dog stopped wiggling and looked at her through ice blue eyes, tail thumping hard, long, pink, tongue lolling out the side of its mouth.

Corey crouched down on the rug and held a hand out for the dog to sniff. "Aren't you a beautiful girl," she gushed and stroked the fuzzy head causing the tail to thump harder and puppy teeth to come down gently on her hand.

Corey popped up when the door opened and Thayer banged back in with two full grocery bags full of supplies, her coat over her nightshirt and boots over bare feet. "Oh, damn, I wanted to be here."

"Oh, thank, god. I thought you had transmogrified."

"Very funny. So, surprise."

Corey blinked at her stupidly and then looked down at the dog, now sitting up and gazing at her adoringly with huge blue eyes, tail thumping wildly. One ear pointed up and the other flopped over. She had soft brown and tan coloring and recognizable open husky mask but with a short, blunt muzzle. "You got me a dog?"

"I got you a dog—*us* a dog She's a chocolate lab-husky mix, on the runty side. She's not expected to be much more than fifty pounds."

Corey was stunned and she and the dog looked at each other again.

"She's seven months old, fully house-trained, and very well behaved as long as she gets enough exercise. Wendy Schilling, the doc who's retiring soon, bought her for her young twin granddaughters for their birthday a few months ago, but it turns out they're allergic. They tried to make it work but she also needs more exercise than they were able to provide. Wendy even sent her to a month of in-home doggie boot camp but it was just never going to be a good fit. I think they're going to try again with something smaller and lazier." Thayer knelt in front of the dog, scratching her ears. "They assure me she's very sweet and playful and a shameless cuddler, but we need to watch for the chewing. Wendy gave me bags of food and toys and I bought a baby gate so we can keep her in the kitchen, at least for now." She finally looked up at Corey. "Are you going to say something?"

Corey opened and closed her mouth a couple of times. "What's her name?"

"It's kind of silly, but the twins named her Charlie Brown Dog."

"Charlie," she repeated and dropped to her knees to go eye to eye with the puppy. "I'm Corey. Would you like to go snowshoeing with me?" She laughed when the puppy's tongue lashed out across her face and her butt wriggled wildly in response.

"And I'm jealous already."

CHAPTER NINE

"Rachel said it was okay to bring Charlie?" Thayer huddled deeper into her coat as they walked slowly down the street in front of the Old Bridge Coffee House letting Charlie do her business.

"It's better to ask for forgiveness than for permission," Corey said. "And as long as Lainey supports me, that's all that matters."

The rest of the downtown street was quiet and dark on Christmas day in contrast with Rachel's shop which was ablaze with lights and warmth that was steaming up the large glass windows in the front. Windows that were now tempered glass instead of plate after a bunch of punks, high on drugs, had thrown bricks through the window injuring several people, including Rachel.

Corey trailed after Charlie as she snuffled along the front of the building and around the corner into the parking lot reserved by Tagliotti, Mancini and Castiglione, the law firm that owned the building and used the top two floors.

She startled when she heard the high-pitched yelp of the puppy and turned the corner only to crash into a heavyset man hurrying through the parking lot. His hat was pulled low and hands jammed into the pockets of a dark parka.

"Hey, watch it, jerk face," she muttered. She stared after him for a long moment certain she recognized him. She bent down to investigate the puppy, who was licking a front paw after apparently having been stepped on.

"You all right?" Thayer asked from the sidewalk staying in the light from the shop.

"Yeah, fine." She ruffled Charlie's ears. She'd already recovered and continued her investigations of the building. Corey glanced up to the second floor to see a single light on. "Looks like someone's working overtime."

"Probably an intern."

"Did you get a look at the guy?" Corey asked, looking down the street at the direction he'd headed. "He seemed really familiar to me."

"No. Sorry." Thayer gave a little shiver. "Ready to head in?"

The front door swung in at Corey's knock and they were greeted drunkenly by Lainey Ortiz, clearly well into her cups. Lainey, Rachel's right-hand woman, was taking over more and more of the day to day operations as the business grew.

Corey described her as if Daria Morgendorffer and Jane Lane had a baby. Her bobbed hair was black and blunt cut. She had chunky glasses and a sharp and merciless sense of humor. She was also a marketing genius and her macchiato brought all the girls to the yard. One of the few things that softened her was her love of animals.

"Corey and Thayer!" she shouted over her shoulder to the room. She ushered them inside, closing and locking the door behind them. She squealed as Charlie skidded in and attacked her feet. "And, oh, my goodness, who is this little darling?"

Corey shrugged out of her coat. "That's Charlie. I hope it's okay."

"Of course, it's okay," Lainey gushed and dropped onto the floor, welcoming the puppy into her lap.

"Merry Christmas, dude." Rachel was grinning at them, her eyes flicking to the puppy. "Is she yours?"

"Yep." Corey held out her fist and Rachel bumped it in greeting. "Christmas gift from Thayer."

"Adorbs." Rachel bent down and ruffled Charlie's ears.

"I'm glad you think so." Corey eyed her expectantly.

"What?"

"Can you watch her for the week we're away?"

"If you were going away you shouldn't have gotten a dog, you dummy."

"I didn't get the dog and Thayer didn't know we were going away. Come on, you love dogs."

"Of course, I'll watch your dog," Rachel said and looked Thayer up and down as she helped her out of her coat and gave her a hug. "This is like Corey's version of a ring, you know? Merry Christmas, gorgeous."

"Merry Christmas, Rachel."

She gestured inside. "Well, come on in. You know everyone."

"This is elaborate," Thayer said.

The tables had been pushed together into one long rectangle. All the guests were still milling about with cocktails, wearing all manner of wildly obnoxious ugly sweaters. The counter was laden with chafing dishes, the sterno keeping the food hot.

"I'm having it catered this year. It used to be just a few of us who couldn't make it home to family or who didn't have family to go home to. Now it's turned into more of a chosen family planned event."

"I love it." Thayer slipped her arm through Corey's and gave it a squeeze before moving around to greet Dana, looking cheerily drunk after having just come off the Christmas day shift.

"Cin, I didn't know you were going to be here," Corey said, offering a hug to Cinnamon James, her friend and occasional assistant in the morgue.

"Merry Christmas, Corey. It wasn't the plan. I saw my family last night but then Audrey hit me back with revisions to my latest dissertation chapter and I have a lot of work to do. I figured I could get more done here. I gotta get this thing finished. I'm either going to defend in the spring or set it on fire—either way I'm over it."

Corey had mixed feelings about Cin finishing her PhD. She was intensely proud of her but knew Cin wasn't going to be on the job market for long and Corey would lose her to a career in academia. "Then what?"

"Not sure. Post doc, maybe, or Cornell may be posting a position soon."

The door chimed again and they turned when Lainey held it open to let in Jude Weatherly with a woman Corey had never seen before on his arm. Last Corey knew, Jude was dating Rachel.

Corey knew Jude as the assistant director of Weatherly's Funeral Home. She had hooked him up with Rachel, and when they had started dating he had also started working at the coffee shop part-time because he enjoyed the vibrancy of it.

"Take it easy," Rachel muttered in Corey's ear. "It's all good. Jude reconnected with his high school flame and he and I had run our course. Everything's fine."

Corey chuckled. "So, you're on the market again?"

"I'm gonna be on the market forever," Rachel replied while she sketched a wave to Jude and his girlfriend. They moved off to meet up with some of the other employees.

Corey and Rachel turned their attention back to the door when it opened again with a blast of cold air.

"Five-O in the house," Lainey announced when a uniformed Kelly Warren stepped in and pulled off his patrol issue beanie, running a hand through his short, messy hair.

Dana shouted. "Holy shit, Rachel, you got a Christmas stripper?"

The room fell silent but for the holiday music over the speakers in the ceiling before Thayer threw her head back and exploded with laughter, the rest of the room joining in.

Dana flushed scarlet to the top of her head when Thayer went over to greet him.

He hugged her back with a mischievous grin before slowly unzipping his coat, slipping it from his shoulders while rolling his hips provocatively.

Corey whistled and Rachel pulled a dollar from her pocket, waving it in front of him while he executed a perfect body roll to the soundtrack of laughter and cheering from the others.

Rachel greeted him when he straightened and hung up his coat. "Hey, Kelly, glad you could make it."

"Oh, you bet." He shook hands with Corey and smiled at the others, his eyes lingering on Dana, who looked like she was trying to sink into the floor and look anywhere but at him. "I can't stay long. I'm on patrol overnight."

"Let me introduce you to my best friend, Dana." Thayer hooked him by the arm. "By the way, do you have any family in town?"

Corey didn't hear the rest of the conversation as they moved over to Dana who was trying to slink away.

"Thayer seems really happy," Rachel said to Corey.

Corey knew her comment was genuine and came from a place of deep love and concern for them. Rachel had seen her share of both Corey and Thayer's roughest moments, the explosive anger and unrelenting tears that followed the bizarre and traumatic events of their first six months as a couple. "Tonight, she is, yeah."

"She's not usually?"

"No, I mean, yeah, she is. The last couple of days have been hit and miss."

"And you've been *missing*?"

"Why do you always gotta think Thayer's moods are my fault?"

Rachel stared at her, blinking and silent.

"Ugh, god. I don't even have a drink yet."

Jude chose that moment to twirl by them, depositing a pink drink with floating cranberries in each of their hands. "Weatherly family tradition—the mistletoe martini." He flitted off as fast he showed up.

Rachel sipped her drink and arched a brow in Corey's direction.

Corey sighed heavily and took a huge swallow of her drink. "We just found out Lil is having financial trouble after her investments shit the bed last year."

"Tell me about it. I'm lucky I got my takeout off the ground before everything shut down or I'd have been shut down forever," Rachel said. "Thayer must be worried."

"She is. Lil's money is tied up in the house, so I offered to buy it."

"One of your more sensible plans."

"I thought so. I'm not so sure Thayer agrees."

"Why?"

"I don't know exactly. Because she had to accept help from someone else? Because she couldn't solve her grandmother's problem on her own? It's all just seemed to shake her confidence again, which doesn't take much after everything. And especially right after what happened the the other night."

"Am I supposed to know what that means?"

Corey shook her head, her teeth grinding at the memory. "These fucking assholes at the Towne Plaza were hassling her and—"

"Oh, shit, wearing all black?"

"You know them?"

"Of them."

"They're not the same idiots that busted out your window, are they?"

"No, but they probably all circle jerk together."

"Is it just me or are there more douche bags in this city per capita? Is anything being done about them?"

"The guys from the bowling alley are Small Business Association members with me. They've been having a lot of trouble with those shitheads. There've been some official complaints, I think, but the police haven't done much." Rachel paused. "What did you do about them?"

"Threatened them with my dollar store ice scraper."

Rachel laughed. "How very restrained of you."

"Tell me about it."

The conversation was interrupted with the clanging of metal when Lainey lifted the lids on the chafing dishes. "Dinner is served!"

CHAPTER TEN

December Twenty-sixth

Thayer was immensely glad she shut herself off early last night as she set a fresh cup of black coffee at the nurses' station in front of Dana. She tried to hide her amusement behind her own mug when Dana looked up, bleary-eyed and pale. "I hope you don't feel as hungover as you look."

Dana slurped her coffee. "Worse. How badly did I embarrass myself last night?"

"You'll need to ask Kelly about that."

"Who?"

Thayer spluttered on her coffee. "No. Dana!"

"I'm kidding." Dana laughed. "Christ, how could I possibly forget? Some friend you are, by the way, keeping him a secret… Oh shit." Her eyes widened at something over Thayer's shoulder.

She turned to see Kelly striding to the desk, thumbs hooked into his duty belt. Her smile faltered at his serious expression. "Uh oh. Why do I get the feeling this isn't a social call?"

"Sorry. I really wish it were." His gaze flicked to Dana and his lip twitched into a quick smile before returning to Thayer.

"I need you to come downstairs with me for a few minutes. Sergeant Collier and I need your help with something."

Thayer frowned. "Downstairs? Why…?" The penny dropped and she sucked in a long breath exhaling slowly. The morgue. "I can't just leave—"

"It's taken care of," he said and gestured toward the door.

She tensed. "What does that mean?"

"Please, Thayer."

She nodded. "Dana, can you get someone else to see my patient—"

"I'm on it. Don't worry." She stood and gathered up a chart giving Thayer an encouraging smile.

"While I appreciate the company, Kelly, what I'd like even more is for you to tell me what the hell is going on," Thayer said as they walked out of the ED. Collier had apparently called up to her director, Dr. Manning, in advance and received permission for her to consult with the police. She was not pleased about him going to her boss before her and her irritation was increasing with every second Kelly did not tell her what this was about. "Is Corey all right?"

"Yes, Corey's fine. Sergeant Collier just asked if I could escort you to the morgue for some questions. I think we should wait for him."

Thayer's heart leapt in her chest. "Jesus, not this again."

"I'm sorry, Thayer," Kelly said before pushing through the door. "I'm sure it's just a misunderstanding."

Thayer smiled weakly at his attempt to ease her mind and placed a hand on his arm. "Thanks, Kelly." She took a deep breath, determined not to assume the worst. "Let's get this over with."

Despite the body on the table in the center of the room, Thayer's eyes immediately sought out Corey's as she straightened off the counter and offered her a wan smile. Thayer returned her smile and hoped she didn't look as unsettled as she felt. The last time she was involved in an investigation it ended with her being assaulted in her own home, the trauma of which still snuck up on her at times and rattled her to the core. She was fairly certain her therapist would frown upon putting herself in similar triggering situations.

She could feel the tension ratcheting up in her neck and jaw. "I'm here. Now, tell me why."

"Thanks for coming down, Doc." Collier flipped open his notebook and gestured to the body. "You recognize him?"

Thayer crossed her arms as she approached the table and cocked her head to peer at his face, icy and blue-tinged. She took a moment and studied the hunkered form and looked at his face again, the hair, the line of his features, his build. She sucked in a breath. "No."

"You sure?" Collier stood, pen poised over his notebook.

"Yes," she replied and looked at Corey for answers but she just stood miserably against the counter. By the set of her shoulders Thayer knew she was feeling the same anxiety. "I don't recognize him. Should I?"

Collier shook out a plastic evidence bag and handed it to her. "How about this?"

Thayer took it, not liking the direction the conversation was going. She dragged her gaze to the paper and her breath hitched with recognition. She took a moment to steady herself before handing the bag back to him. "That's my signature and license number from a prescription I wrote."

"Can you tell me when?"

"The date says December twenty-fourth."

"What did you write it for?"

Thayer sighed deeply and stared at the ceiling for a moment. "Without knowing to whom I wrote it; I can't be certain."

"Okay, *to whom* did you write it?"

"I can't be certain."

Collier looked up from his notebook and pointed to the body with his pen. "But not to him."

"I told you I don't recognize him."

"Do you remember all your patients?"

"Do you remember everyone you arrest?"

"Let's not start this again, Doc," Collier said calmly and closed his notebook. "You're not in any trouble. I've got an unidentified dead body with your name in his pocket. I'm just looking for some help here."

Thayer exhaled slowly and tried to relax. "I wrote that script Christmas Eve. We were busy, but I only worked noon to six. This man was not one of my patients that day. Of that, I am certain."

"Great. That helps. Any idea who I should be looking for? Who the owner of that script is?"

Thayer pressed her lips together in a thin line and looked at the body, directing her next question to Corey. "Do you know how he died?"

Corey shook her head. "No visible trauma but he's so frozen I can't even get fluids for a tox screen right now."

Thayer looked back at Collier. "Is the death suspicious?"

"Hell, yeah, it's suspicious. I got a frozen body found under a dumpster near the Towne Plaza."

"I guess what I mean is, do you suspect foul play? Is that the correct phrase?"

"Nothing I can prove but my gut tells me a young guy like this didn't just curl up in the snow and go to sleep."

She arched a brow. "If he was under the influence perhaps that's exactly what happened."

"Okay, fine." Collier's patience appeared to be running out. "But based on the fact that you did not write that prescription for him, and assuming he didn't just find it, we have credible evidence that someone else interacted with this guy before he died. Do you know who that person is?"

"Unless you can tell me that my patient is suspected of committing a crime or his life is in danger, I can't reveal information about him."

"He?" Collier's eyes narrowed. "So, you do know who it is?"

"I told you. I can't be certain."

"Best guess, Doc."

Thayer shook her head, working to control her rising frustration. "I'm not just going to shout out names of my patients on the chance that one of them is the person you're looking for."

"I can go to Manning."

"Do that. And he can tell you the same thing. Patient confidentiality is protected—by law."

If possible, the room got chillier. Kelly Warren shifted back and forth uncomfortably. "Is there anything you can do to help us, Thayer?"

Thayer's gaze flicked to him and she felt some of the fight go out of her. "Okay, look, Jim, I'm sorry. I'm not trying to make your job more difficult. Can you give me some time and let me think about the implications of this? Maybe let me speak with Dr. Manning or the Legal department?"

Collier relaxed, visibly. "How long?"

Thayer sucked in a breath through her teeth, considering. "Do you have a card on you?"

"You know my number," he replied suspiciously.

She held out her hand. "Please?"

He pulled a card from a case in an inner breast pocket and handed it over. "I don't like this, Doc."

"If you don't have any other information in a couple days I'll see what I can do, okay?"

"Well, you don't leave me much choice." His eyes flicked to Corey. "Can't you just nuke the guy or something to speed this up?"

Corey shook her head. "He's frozen, man, what do you want me to say? The only thing keeping him from decomposing is the temperature. I try to warm him up and his outside starts to rot before his insides are thawed. It'll fuck up the case six ways from Sunday. Already we're going to be dealing with ice crystals in all the tissues, which is going to cause problems."

"How long? Ballpark?"

"Give me a minute." She snapped gloves back on and yanked open drawers until she found a long thermometer. She spread apart the body's buttocks with obvious effort—the tissue rigid and unforgiving—probing with a gloved finger for the anal sphincter. She patted his cheek as she slid the thermometer deep into his rectum "Sorry, buddy, I feel you. This takes *corpsicle* to a whole new level."

Kelly Warren stepped closer to watch. "You don't use a liver probe or something?"

"What? No, that's stupid."

"It doesn't work?"

"No, it works, but intentionally putting a hole through the gut of a body whose death is already suspicious is a terrible idea. You have no idea what you could be damaging. They just show that shit on television 'cause shoving a thermometer up a dead guy's ass is a lot less sexy for primetime."

Thayer looked away, her nerves on the ragged edge, her teeth grinding again.

"Well?" Collier asked when Corey removed the thermometer with an unceremonious jerk.

"Twenty-five degrees." She tossed the instrument into the sink. "Which is about on par with how cold it's been outside and considering he's been near room temperature for a couple hours."

"So, what do you think?" Collier asked impatiently.

"Well, I don't have a whole lot of experience with this but I'd say three or four days."

"Christ," Collier growled. He pulled his phone and stabbed in a number. "I gotta make some calls."

Corey turned to Thayer. "If they're not expecting you back right away I can pack this guy up in the cooler and we can get a cup of coffee."

"What? No, I don't want to get coffee."

Corey frowned. "I was just—"

"I've had enough. You just do whatever it is you do. I need to get back to work." She stalked out.

"Thayer, hold up." Corey yanked off her gloves and ripped off her plastic apron on the run and banged out the door after her. "Wait, damn it." She caught up with her just outside the door and placed a hand on her arm when she showed no signs of slowing down.

Thayer spun at Corey's touch and backed away from her. "Don't touch me."

Corey's heart lurched at the anger in her tone and she raised her hands. "I'm sorry. Please, talk to me."

"I have to get back to work."

"Thayer, what's going on? I mean, I get that what just happened in there was tough for you. It brought up a ton of shit for me too, but why do I feel like your anger has more to do with me than with that body?"

"I didn't realize you were so..." Thayer frowned at her and gestured dismissively. "...cavalier about it all, I guess."

"I wouldn't call it that. I know my sense of humor runs dark, but I'm eviscerating him not eulogizing him."

Thayer crossed her arms tightly as if she were cold. "They're people, Corey, and they should be respected, not treated like a gruesome joke around the water cooler."

"Wait, what? A joke? That's not...They're people when you see them, Thayer. When I see them it's the bodies those people left behind when they died."

"I don't need a philosophical lecture from you based on your twisted ideas on death."

"Twisted? Are you serious right now?"

"I've seen you show more compassion assembling an Ikea cabinet." Thayer gestured toward the morgue door. "Is this all just some sort of fun game for you with cool stories to tell your friends over a beer?"

"Thayer." Corey breathed deeply, her jaw clenching in anger at being judged so harshly. "I don't know what you expected. Yeah, what I do to most people is probably macabre, at best. Maybe I come across as cold or casual, but I am good at my job. I get answers and closure for families. And make no mistake, my detachment or my commentary is not for lack of respect or compassion."

Thayer jammed her hands in the pockets of her white coat. "Whatever, Corey."

"No, not *whatever*, Thayer. Because last week was a post on Mason, Baby Boy B. He lived for three minutes after a cord vessel rupture during labor. He got a birth certificate and death certificate at the same time. His twin brother made it but is still in the NICU. It could get me fired for violating the privacy laws you hold so dear but I've been following along with his progress to make sure his parents get to take one of their babies home."

Thayer looked away, her shoulders dropping. "I didn't mean to—"

"Not to, you know, go all Erin Brockovich, but two years ago was Andrews, Ethan, twenty-three-year-old graduate student who got run over by a dumptruck one afternoon on his bike while on his way to campus. He was an only child that took his parents six years of fertility treatments to conceive. I don't know why that was in the report but I know that about him. He was their miracle child."

"Corey, stop, please."

"I'm not done. Back in October there was Schaefer, Constance, forty-seven years old and morbidly obese. She came in to the hospital for a partial left foot amputation due to a nonhealing diabetic ulcer. There were no beds available for her post-op so they roomed her in the pediatric wing overnight. She died of positional obstructive asphyxia because the staff on the peds floor didn't know she should be sleeping inclined." Corey shrugged, dramatically. "Oops. She left behind a husband and three teenagers. There's going to be a big payout on that one but their mom is still dead. You want me to go on?"

"No," Thayer whispered, clearly fighting tears. "I didn't mean to…I should never have said…I'm sorry."

"Yeah." Corey's anger drained out of her as she turned away, pushing back through the door. "Me, too."

Collier was standing in the ante room on the other side of the door. "Everything all right?"

"I'm sure you could hear just fine."

"Sounds like what you and Doc got is a failure to communicate."

She leaned against the table on her hands and glared at him across the body. "No, she's got it all figured out. I'm just cold-blooded."

"Don't be a dick, Curtis. You know damn we'll she doesn't think that."

"You heard her."

"What I heard was a woman lashing out in fear, at a safe target. Someone she trusts to understand and forgive her because she's rattled about just being questioned by the police about a suspicious death—again."

Corey stared slack jawed. "Yeah, thanks, Dr. Phil."

"Think about it for a minute."

"Thayer is strong and she knows her own mind. She's always been the first person to know when she needs help."

"I'm not the one that needs to be reminded of that. But if you think she's not still deeply affected by what happened, you haven't been paying attention. So, maybe you listen less to what she's saying and figure out what she's not."

Corey gaped comically. "Who the hell are you and what have you done with Collier?"

"Tell me I'm wrong."

Corey blinked at him. She was unable to come up with an effective argument. Everything he said made perfect sense and her anger at Thayer turned to worry in an instant. And shame at the deliberately upsetting things she had said. "Shit."

"Don't sweat it, Curtis. I would have popped off exactly like that at anyone questioning my professional integrity—including Austin. 'Course, I woulda been wrong, too."

"Thanks a lot," she muttered.

"For what it's worth, from someone who's worked this gig a long time, I've never seen anyone do what you do with as much class. Even though your jokes are stupid."

She snorted a laugh. "Jesus Christ, man, what has Steph been feeding you?"

"Fucking kale and queen-wa."

"Quinoa." She grabbed a sheet to cover the body.

"Whatever. Doesn't Doc make you eat that shit?"

"Hell, no."

"I'm coming over for dinner."

CHAPTER ELEVEN

Corey started the Range Rover to let it warm while she took the scraper to the windows. It had drizzled in the afternoon followed by dropping temperatures. She was chipping away at the windshield when she heard Thayer crunch her way across the parking lot.

"Corey."

"Hey. Be done in a minute. Get in and get warm." When Thayer didn't move, Corey turned.

Her face was rosy from the cold even in the short walk from the ED entrance. Her shoulders were hunched and her hands jammed into the pockets of her long wool coat, and though she wouldn't meet Corey's eyes, Corey could see her sadness.

She dropped the scraper and crossed the short distance pulling Thayer into her arms and holding her tight. "I'm sorry, babe. I was an insensitive asshole and I—"

"No, Corey, no." Her arms came up around Corey's waist. "You are good and unwavering. You do amazing work that so few people would understand or appreciate, let alone do themselves.

I'm so sorry I made you feel otherwise and I should never have said—"

"Hush, woman." Corey pulled away to see her golden eyes glittering with unshed tears. She placed a warm kiss on her lips. "Don't worry about me. Let's talk at home."

Corey didn't bother with her boots and went right to the kitchen and froze when she saw the gate askew, the dog bed in pieces and Charlie nowhere to be found. "Oh, shit," she whispered.

"I'm going to take a shower." Thayer hung up her coat and kicked out of her boots.

"Great." Corey leaned against the counter doing her best to block the carnage. "Are you hungry?"

"Yes. Anything, thank you." She headed down the hall. "Please, find the puppy and clean up any mess she made."

"Charlie!" Corey hissed. "Get your little ass over here."

The puppy slunk out from the great room, whining pitifully as she dropped a mangled shoe at Corey's feet. It was Thayer's.

"You're going to get us both in trouble." She tried to be angry, but huge blue eyes stared longingly at her and her tail began to thump. She caved and ruffled her ears and Charlie wriggled with pleasure at the attention. "Get outside while I clean up your mess. We'll have to cuddle later." She held the door for her and the puppy took off into the snow, racing around the dark yard. She wasn't worried. After only a couple days they had bonded pretty strongly and Charlie never went far without her. Corey disappeared the shoe and the bed stuffing and did a quick sweep of the house for any other evidence of misbehavior— which she stepped in.

Following the cleanup she stared into the fridge. The ride home had been quiet. Corey had flicked her glance from the road to Thayer, but she was somewhere far away as she looked out the window and Corey hated the distance she felt between them. She reached across the physical space to place her hand on Thayer's leg. She didn't speak but covered Corey's hand with her own, and that had been enough.

She turned up her nose at the idea of Christmas leftovers from Rachel's party. It had all been wonderful but they had been eating it for two days. She quickly assessed her other options and what at first glance looked like an array of cheeses and condiments turned into loaded nachos.

Corey built up the fire while her pan of nachos was heating and by the time Thayer returned in lounge pants and T-shirt with a towel in hand, Corey had opened a couple of beers and moved the food to a plate and set everything up in front of the fire. Charlie, cold and damp from the snow, was back in the kitchen, her face buried in her kibble and an old sheet repurposed for her bed.

Thayer spun down onto the bearskin rug to sit cross-legged in front of the fire and Corey descended far less gracefully and mirrored her position. She placed the nachos between them and smiled when Thayer's face lit up at her impromptu creation.

They ate quietly for several minutes until Corey asked. "Will you tell me about it?"

"Nothing to tell."

Corey didn't challenge her right away, instead watching how the firelight danced in her eyes.

It had only been four months since Thayer was assaulted. Regardless of her strength, self-care, and therapy, Corey still saw the shadows of her shaken confidence from time to time.

"Please, talk to me. I know this must have brought up feelings."

Thayer flinched, and Corey could see her throat working hard to swallow. "I just feel so out of control right now."

"Out of control of what?" Corey asked softly.

"Everything. That scene with Nana and her financial situation and feeling helpless to fix it or ease her worry. Then talking about what happened with my parents, and god, now this. I just don't have room to worry about one more thing and I really don't want to get…"

"Get what?" Corey encouraged when she trailed off.

"Set back," she finally said, staring at the fire.

"Does it help to know that I believe, with every fiber of my being, that you are strong and courageous and capable. I know, better than anyone, whatever challenges you face you take on with grace, dignity, and patience."

Thayer took a shuddering breath, the tears that had been threatening spilled over and shone in the firelight as they tracked down her face. "Yes, of course it helps."

"But it's not enough, is it?"

Thayer turned to her finally, not trying to hide her grief. "Oh, sweetheart, you have no idea what that means to me and how much I wish it were. But I need to figure out some way to feel like I've taken back control over my life, so that every little thing that happens doesn't send me spiraling back into this feeling of helplessness."

"I will do everything I can to help you do that. You know that, right?"

Thayer smiled through her tears and swiped a hand across her cheeks. "I know. A week in Key West with you will be an amazing start. I can't tell you how much I'm looking forward to that."

"That's still over a week away. What can I do right now?"

"Will you just hold me for a while?"

Corey moved the food and beer back to the table and stacked the floor pillows behind her before opening her arms for Thayer.

She moved in, her back to Corey, and Corey circled her waist with her arms and leaned them back against the pillows in front of the fire.

Corey could feel Thayer's heart beating against her chest, steady and slow, and her still damp, lavender-smelling hair tickled her nose as her head rested against Corey's shoulder. She knew she would do whatever she could to support Thayer, but she hated that she couldn't do more.

Thayer's eyes flew open on a shuddering gasp and she sat bolt up in bed, her hand going to her chest.

The nightmare was dark and vague, nothing like the first months where his face had loomed in her mind's eye, his voice echoing in her ears. This enemy was nameless and faceless and lived in her own heart, twisting her head with uncertainty and doubt. "Shit," she breathed and dropped her head into her hands, smoothing damp hair from her face.

"Thayer?" Corey sat up and reached for her. "Are you all right?"

She took several steadying breaths. "I need to do something."

Corey turned on the bedside light. "About what?"

"About that body. About my patient."

"You *do* know who you wrote that script for."

"Of course, I do. Why do you think I asked for Jim's card? I need to talk to my patient."

"That's not a good idea," Corey warned. "If you want to do something you should tell Collier and let him proceed with the investigation."

Thayer shook her head, fiercely. "No, absolutely not. There's no reason to think he's done anything wrong. Jim said so himself and I'm not giving his name to the police."

"I get that, babe, I do. I get that you want to help and you want to take back some power over this, but I don't think you should get involved in this any more than you already are."

"You said you would do everything you could to help me. Please, mean that."

"Damn it, Thayer." Corey exhaled and shook her head, running her hands through her hair. "We already know from experience how this plays out, and at best we get in Collier's way and one of us spends a night in jail—me probably. At worst, one of us gets hurt—again."

"Those are not the only possible outcomes. I'm not talking about interfering with a police investigation and right now there's no reason to think there's any danger. The cause of death is exposure most likely, right?"

"Please, just try and let it go."

"Like *you* let it go? Twice?"

"That's not fair. I never intentionally planned to—"

"You nearly got yourself killed, Corey. You nearly got me—" She sucked in a sharp breath as she watched the color drain from Corey's face.

"There it is," Corey said tightly.

"I didn't mean that."

"So, I owe you, is that it? You know, I don't even think you're wrong. I live with that every day. But I sure as hell am not going to repay my debt by walking you right into some other fucked up situation with the potential for one of us to wind up on a steel table."

Thayer moved over to Corey as close as she could without touching her. She could feel the hurt in the air between them. "I am sorry. You don't owe me anything, sweetheart. None of what has happened was your fault."

"Are you sure you really believe that?"

"With all my heart, and I should never have suggested otherwise."

"There's a 'but' coming. I can feel it."

Thayer's mouth quirked up. "We are wonderfully different in ways too many to name. And the ways we are the same, the core values we share that bind us together, are fewer but run deep. Our worldviews, our moral compass, the deal breakers and the unforgivables. Our belief in right and wrong, our desire to protect, help and heal in whatever ways we can. Our need for answers and solutions to problems. It's how we met and what's helped bring us closer. I know you understand what I'm saying and I know you believe it."

"Of course, I understand, but that doesn't mean we need to run off like lunatics every time a mystery presents itself." Corey huffed a breath. "And how the hell am I the voice of reason right now?"

Thayer stared at her for a long time. "Oh, god, you're right. It's crazy and I'm being totally melodramatic, aren't I? I have no right to ask you to involve yourself in fresh shenanigans that could upset Jim or get you in trouble for what will probably amount to alcohol intoxication and hypothermia."

Corey's brow furrowed and she looked away. "Probably."

"Probably."

"It's a terrible idea, Thayer."

"Totally, yes, I hear you. You are absolutely correct."

Corey was quiet a long time before picking up a pillow, smothering her face into it and howling unintelligibly what Thayer could only assume was a string of profanity.

She schooled her expression and waited for Corey to work through whatever inner turmoil seemed to have overtaken her. She tried not to look hopeful when Corey removed the pillow and looked up. Her face was beet red and she was out of breath.

"Shenanigans? Is that what we're calling it now?"

Thayer shrugged. "What would you call it?"

"I'm going to tell Collier. I'm not doing this behind his back."

"Tell him what?"

"Tell him you're going to get in touch with the patient you think he's looking for and that *you* will tell him to call Collier. In the event the patient will not contact Collier, *you* will provide Collier with his name."

"Agreed. Is that a *yes*?"

"I assume you know how to find this patient, and your plan is go and talk to him after work? Under the pretense of a house call, perhaps?"

"Why would you assume that?"

"Because that's what I would do."

CHAPTER TWELVE

Corey stood in the cooler, her cell tucked between her shoulder and her ear and the thermometer buried inside the bowels of the body. "Cin, I know you're busy and I know Audrey is away at a conference, but I need a favor."

"I figured."

"What? Why, what do you know?"

"I know you hate talking on the phone and never call me unless you need something, to start."

Corey frowned. "That's not true. Is it?"

"It's all good. What do you need, Corey?"

"I need to borrow the handheld X-ray."

"When?"

"As soon as you can. Now."

"Give me a bit. I'm not on campus," Cin said.

"I so owe you."

"You're right, you do."

She pulled the thermometer out and her phone slipped from her ear and clattered to the floor. "Fuck."

She was still cleaning her phone down with a disinfectant wipe when the buzzer sounded. "That was fast," she muttered.

She flung the door open and was blasted with a cacophony of noise from the loading dock. Car doors slammed, an ambulance rumbled in with lights still on, and at least half a dozen plainclothes and uniformed police shouted into phones and at each other. The sense of urgency was so extreme she wondered if they were in the right place. Dead people didn't usually generate this kind of activity. "The fuck?"

"I gotta call Webster," Collier barked as he shouldered past her.

"Why? What the hell is going on?"

"Marcus Bright was found dead in his car by his wife this morning. Gunshot wound to the head," Detective Steph Austin said as she came up the loading dock steps.

Corey's mouth gaped. "Marcus Bright, the town councilman?"

"And recently announced mayoral candidate." Steph gave her arm a squeeze. "Sorry about the circus."

Corey watched as they unloaded the body, the other officers hovering around. Up the hill from the loading dock, a couple of news vans pulled along the curb. "Jesus Christ."

"Yeah, I know. But when a prominent city figure and pillar of the community is executed in his own driveway, people tend to take notice."

"Is this a narcotics case?" Corey asked and held the door, nodding a greeting to two more detectives, David Janus and Carol Linney, from homicide, who preceded the paramedics with the gurney and black bodybag.

"It's pretty much all hands on deck until we get a handle on what's going on and why something like this would happen." Steph blew out a long breath. "How's Thayer doing? Jim told me they had a...conversation yesterday."

"Uh, she's good, I think."

"You think?"

"No, I mean, yeah, she's good. She's got a lot going on right now and she's kind of spinning, but we're good."

"Heard she got you a puppy for Christmas."

Corey's expression brightened. "Oh, yeah. Charlie. You gotta come by and meet her."

"I would love to. Is there a dinner invitation in the offer?"

"Yes, totally. I'll mention it to Thayer. We'll set something up for when we come back from vacation." Corey hissed a breath when she saw Cin pull in, squeezing her car into a nonexistent spot. "Oh, shit."

"I better get inside." Steph disappeared through the door.

"Hey, Cin." Corey waited for her to grab the black case of the portable X-ray out of the car.

"What's going on here?"

"Total bedlam. Any chance we can reschedule for later?"

"No. I've got a meeting with my writing group in an hour to go over my revisions." Cin shivered. "It's freezing. Why are we standing out here?"

Corey held the door for her and led the way back into the autopsy suite. Collier was just hanging up the phone and the rest of the crowd shuffled around in the limited space while the paramedics transferred the bodybag to the autopsy table, wheeled the gurney back out the door and went on with their day.

"Webster's on his way down," Collier said. "Let's get started."

"I need to talk to you about the frozen guy," Corey said.

Collier was already studying notes in his book and didn't look up. "He thaw out?"

"No, but his temp is—"

"Doc going to give me a name?"

"I don't…no, I don't think so but—"

"Then, what's to talk about?"

"Cin's going to do a scan with the portable X-ray for us."

"That all?"

"Well, I talked to Thayer about it and she said—"

"He's not even out of the bag yet?" The door banged open and Randall Webster lumbered in cutting her off. He gave Corey a look suggesting he thought she was wasting his time.

"We're going now." Collier moved from the anteroom. "Curtis?"

"Be right there." She smiled apologetically at Cin who was unpacking the camera on Corey's desk. "Can you do it in the cooler?"

"Seriously, Corey?"

"I know, I'm sorry. I'll—"

"Curtis!" Collier bellowed.

"Fuck. Sorry." Corey winced and left Cin grumbling to herself.

She handed out booties to the others and gloved and gowned before unzipping the bag. Marcus Bright had been a good looking, fit, fifty-year-old man. His hair was shaved to the scalp which made the destruction of a bullet through his head all the more dramatic with a neat entry hole at his left temple and a jagged, blown apart exit wound the size of her palm above his right ear. The skull fragments, still attached to the skin, opened like a gruesome flower with chunks of brain and blood sticking to the side of his face.

Webster eyed the wounds. "Not much mystery around cause of death. You find the bullet?"

"Officers and forensics are going over the scene still," Collier said, scribbling away.

"His wife found him, you say?" Webster stood back while Corey rolled the body back and forth to work the bag out from under him.

"She said he left for work at his usual time," Steph answered. "She assumed he had gone when she heard the shot a few minutes later and came out of the house to find him dead in his car behind the wheel. She didn't see anyone else."

Corey took pictures from above, first, getting him in the full frame in his carefully tailored suit, now blood and brain splattered. "So, someone was just lying in wait for him and approached the car, putting a bullet through his brain?"

Collier replied, "That's what we're going to find out."

"Did they shoot through the window? I don't see any glass." She hopped off the stool and began to undress him, tie first.

"Window was down."

Corey considered this and pointed to the circle of black powder at his temple. "There's stippling around the entry wound, so obviously close range and it's freezing out. So, you think he knew the killer and put the window down to speak with them?"

"Stay in your lane, Curtis," Collier snapped.

"Sorry, Christ." She focused on the task at hand, undressing the body and getting pictures of everything. She moved around the table, rolling his body when necessary and pulling his clothes off, leaving them as intact as possible and placing each item into a separate evidence bag Detective Janus held out for her.

"What do you think about the size of that entry wound, Dr. Webster?" Detective Linney asked. "A .45?"

Webster looked closer at both entry and exit wounds. "Could be."

Corey pulled the sleeve of his white shirt down his left arm, jerking it over his hand and frowning as a new smear of blood bloomed through the fabric. She pulled the shirt all the way off, dropping it in the bag held out to her. She picked the arm back up, studying the hand more closely. "Uh oh," she murmured.

"What?" Collier looked up and all eyes turned to her.

"Anyone know if Marcus Bright was left handed?"

"He was," Janus said. "Saw him throw the first pitch out at the River Rats opener last year."

She held up the hand so the others could see the fresh, linear laceration in the webbing of his left hand. "What's that look like to you?"

Collier leaned forward, his eyes narrowing. "Slide bite," he growled when he identified the common injury when firing a handgun with improper grip. "Goddamn it."

No one spoke for several moments as they all understood the implications.

"Linney, find out if Bright has a handgun registered in his name," Colllier barked.

"On it." She disappeared into the anteroom, pulling out her phone.

"Austin, go back and talk to his wife. If she found him and she picked up the gun to cover a suicide for whatever reason, we need to know, now. And find the gun."

"Janus, get those clothes to forensics and let the team going through the car know we may be looking for evidence that the gun dropped in the car for a time. There may be burns in the upholstery or the floor mats or his pants. And get forensics at the scene to test Mrs. Bright's hands and get down here to test the body."

"Yep." Janus gathered up the bagged clothes and disappeared with the others, leaving Collier with Webster and Corey.

"Well?" Collier said.

"Well, what?" Webster was measuring the entry and exit wounds with a set of calipers while Corey took notes.

"Can you prove suicide?"

"We can perform the postmortem and provide you with details on angle of entry and exit and most likely scenarios. The rest is your job, Sergeant."

"You can't give me anything now?"

Webster's face went through a strange series of expressions. "Corey, will you close the tissue up on that exit wound?"

She carefully folded the bone and skin back into place, so the hole blown in his skull could be more clearly seen.

Webster looked back and forth from the entry to exit and took a few measurements with the calipers from the wounds to the crown of his head. "The exit wound is slightly higher than the entry wound, suggesting the gun was angled up. Unlikely if there was an average-size assailant standing outside the vehicle firing down on him. We'll be more precise after tracking the path of the bullet. Additionally, I would posit, if the window was down and he was speaking to someone on the outside, who then shot him, his head would have been turned toward the outside, placing the entry wound more anterior on his skull."

"Why put the window down at all, then?" Corey asked.

"To give himself a better entry angle," Webster replied.

Collier was scribbling furiously in his book. "Christ, I gotta update the brass."

"Corey?" Cin stood in the doorway, the camera already back in the case.

"Excuse me." Corey ducked out. "Anything?"

"Nada." Cin shrugged back into her coat. "Some fillings but that's all."

"Okay. I didn't really expect anything but I wanted to be sure."

"I have to go. I'll email you the images."

"Thanks, Cin, you're the best." Corey closed the door behind her as Collier headed into the anteroom stabbing hard at his phone, eye twitching madly indicating his level of anger.

"Collier, I need to talk to you about—" She sighed when he cut her off with a wave of his hand and started shouting orders into his phone and putting his coat on at the same time.

She gritted her teeth and waited for him to hang up. "Jesus, can you give me a minute, please?"

"Not now, Curtis. I got half the goddamn force out scouring the city for a nonexistent murderer and the Loo wants a press conference and I gotta get back to the scene."

She followed him out to the loading dock while he made another call and shouted some more while getting into his car. "Thayer and I are going to talk to her patient after work and see if we can get him to call you about what he might know about the frozen body," she yelled at him. "Hope that's okay."

He didn't look at her, sketching a wave as he backed out, tires squealing.

"Good talk," Corey muttered and headed back inside.

The case was too high profile for anyone but Dr. Webster to handle, and Corey was all too happy to be relegated to assistant while Webster performed a textbook en bloc evisceration and dissection.

It was better this way. As distracted as she was, she was making mistakes simply recording the weights of the man's kidneys. Marcus Bright's tragic death deserved someone's undivided attention. As long as she could think of nothing but helping Thayer, Marcus Bright would have to be someone else's problem.

CHAPTER THIRTEEN

"Hi, sweetheart." Thayer gave Corey a quick kiss when she climbed into the passenger seat of her SUV, idling in a fifteen-minute visitor's spot. "How was your day?"

"It was a little crazy, actually. You?"

"Good." Thayer smiled, feeling more centered than she had been since she got called down to the morgue. "I did good work today. What did Jim say when you told him about our intended shenanigans?"

"Well, I didn't really get a chance to speak with him about it. That was part of the crazy."

"Oh, did it have to do with the death of Marcus Bright? It was all over the news. His poor family."

"Yep."

"They didn't give much information but it all sounds terrible. Do you know how he died?"

"Yep."

"I guess you would." Thayer placed a hand on her knee and squeezed. "I'll stop asking."

Corey stopped at the intersection that took them out of the hospital. "It's just occurred to me that I don't know where we're going."

Thayer inhaled deeply. Despite their reasons for going, she felt oddly relaxed at the thought of the destination. It had been years since she'd been to church outside of weddings and funerals. No matter the occasion it was always a place she felt safe despite what individual members of any particular religion or congregation felt about her right to be there. Her relationship with God didn't have anything to do with anyone else and she didn't need anyone's permission. "We're going to church."

Corey's brows rose. "That is not what I expected you to say."

"Jackson City Unitarian Universalist Church."

"The one that used to be St. Joseph's Catholic? I have no idea how I know that. I know where it is." Corey's text alert stopped her from commenting further and she dug in her pocket for her phone.

Thayer snatched it out of her hand. "I'll do that, you just drive. It's Rachel."

"What's it say?"

"Mother fuck fuck. Frankie's."

"Great," Corey muttered.

"What does that mean?"

"That's like Rachel's version of 911. You mind if we swing by there?"

"Where exactly? Who's Frankie?" she asked while she texted a reply. "More importantly, can I get a coffee there?"

The door jingled from an old school bell overhead when Thayer pushed it open. She looked around wide-eyed at the framed art in the entryway of Frankie Fortune Tattoo and Piercing, which was just a few blocks down from the coffee shop.

"Make yourself comfortable," a woman's voice called from the back over the drone of an intermittent, high-pitched buzzing.

"Wow," Thayer whispered, slipping out of her coat and draping it over her arm as they entered a warm and welcoming waiting area. There was a nice area rug over top of black-and-white tiled floor. There was a coffee maker on the glass topped counter of the display case burbling away with wonderful smelling freshly brewed coffee. A stack of large paper cups and lids sat next to it along with all the usual fixings. "May I?" She glanced to Corey for permission.

"That's what it's there for."

Thayer peered inside the case to see a wide array of jewelry for piercings while she fixed her coffee. Her gaze flicked to Corey who was watching her with a small smile on her face. "What?" she asked.

"I'm just curious what your reaction is to this place."

"And does my reaction meet with your approval?" Thayer asked and moved around the walls to study the photographs of freshly-tattooed skin. "Are all of these hers?"

"Mostly. She has guest artists from time to time."

"These are so beautiful," she mused, moving from image to image of black and gray pieces to photo realistic color to traditional Japanese. "I guess I expected it to be more, hmm, mundane maybe? Or common? I don't know the language."

"Frankie only does custom work by appointment, so you won't see any of the usual flash images."

"Flash?"

"The generic pre-drawn images on the walls popular with the first-timers."

"Ah, okay." Thayer continued her perusal, her interest piqued in a way she would never have guessed. She loved Corey's tattoo. It was meaningful to her and embodied an aspect of her personality that was important to her. Rachel's tattoos practically told her life story. Their body art was as much a part of who they were as their eye color—more so even, as it was intentional.

The buzzing cut off abruptly and the woman called out again. "Corey, if that's you, you can come on back. We're almost done."

"You wanna check it out?" Corey gestured toward the doorway strung with intricate, beaded bamboo curtains.

"It's okay?" Thayer was surprised how excited she was to see. At Corey's nod she parted the beads as gently as possible and stepped into a larger room lit as brightly as the best OR.

Rachel was reclining on what looked more or less like a dentist's exam chair with her right arm propped up on a padded stand. Frankie, Thayer assumed, was hunkered over her forearm, the tattoo machine held in her right hand like a pen. In her left hand was a folded paper towel she occasionally swiped across Rachel's skin, wiping away blood and excess ink.

As comfortable as the chair looked, Rachel looked anything but relaxed as she texted furiously with her left hand. Her face was so pinched Thayer wondered how much getting a tattoo really hurt. Either that or there really was an emergency.

"Fuck. Fuck. Shit." Rachel cocked her arm back as if to hurl her phone across the room.

"Don't move, Rachel," Frankie said.

"What's going on?" Corey asked. "That is not the face of a woman getting her favorite vampire pin-up girl touched up."

"I am up shit's creek right now," Rachel replied, her head dropping back against the chair.

"Love that show."

"Don't even joke, dude. My band for New Year's just shit the bed. Like, literally, had a holiday blowup and broke up. They just cancelled on me."

"So, get someone else."

"Yeah, thanks, asshole. That's what I'm trying to do, but the party is days away and everyone is booked. I need help."

"You think I just keep a band in my back pocket? I can make you a playlist."

Frankie snorted a laugh but continued working, head down.

Rachel sighed dramatically. "It's not a goddamn frat party, Corey. The Women's Business Association is going to be there and so are members of the Chamber of Commerce and other important city people whose support I will need if I ever want to expand. I can't have a playlist."

"You're expanding? Cool, 'cause a coffee truck at the hospital would be amazeballs."

Rachel glowered.

"I can ask around at work, if that helps," Thayer offered apologetically. "Beyond that I can't really think of what I can do for you."

"Shit." Rachel raked her free hand through her hair in a move nearly indentical to Corey's. "I'm fucked."

Corey looked helplessly at Thayer who tapped her watch in response. "Rach, I'm sorry but we have plans to be somewhere. Can I call you tomorrow?"

"Yeah, sure, whatever. Where are you two off to anyway?"

"The UU church," Thayer said.

Rachel raised her head from the chair, her eyes brightening. "Reverend Nora Warren's church? Kelly's sister?"

"Kelly's sister?" Corey blurted. "Wait, what?"

"I hadn't mentioned that part yet," Thayer said and looked to Rachel. "Do you know her?"

"By reputation only. Every month at least half a dozen requests are for a concert to benefit AllWays House, the LGBTQ youth shelter she directs. I've been busy with some new community ideas and I've turned over the charity scheduling to Lainey, and as queer as she is, she totally has her own agenda which usually involves baby animals." Rachel pursed her lips in thought. "But now I have a new idea."

"What?" Corey tried to hurry the conversation along.

"She owns a church and where there's a church there's likely music," Rachel said gleefully.

"Mmm, I doubt very much she owns the church," Thayer corrected.

"Whatever. I'm coming with you."

"No, you're not," Corey said and gestured to Frankie. "And you're busy."

"Done." Frankie switched off the machine and cleaned up Rachel's arm before smearing her skin with ointment. "All good? I had to be careful around the skin here." She pointed to the thin crisscrossing healed scars from when Rachel was cut when drugged out punks threw a brick through her coffee shop's front window. "So, the lines aren't as smooth as they once were, but unless someone is really looking hard, you'll never be able to tell."

Rachel studied her forearm and nodded, a slow smile spreading. "She's smokin' once again. Thanks, Frankie."

"You bet, girl." Frankie stood and stretched her back, her gaze taking in Corey and Thayer. "What's good, Corey? When you gonna let me get my hands on your body again?"

"When I'm feeling inspired again, I guess." She turned to Thayer. "Frankie, this is Thayer."

Frankie smiled, showing off dimples and straight white teeth against smooth, olive skin. Large brown eyes sized Thayer up from behind dark round glasses. She was as tall as Corey, but thinner. They looked like they shopped in the same jeans and faded T-shirt department.

She was wonderfully unconventional with quarter-size spacers in her ears and her dark hair dyed bright blue and cut short in a wide swath across the top and back and shaved down to skin at the sides.

Thayer extended her hand and noticed both her arms were covered in intricate, almost filigree like designs of foliage extending over her hands. "Very pleased to meet you, Frankie."

"You, too," Franking replied meeting her hand with her strong, warm grip. "I don't suppose I can interest you in spending some time in my chair?"

"Well, to be honest, I never really considered it. Your shop is very intriguing and your artwork wonderful," Thayer said.

Frankie's smile widened. "I'm honored."

"You thinking about getting inked, Thayer?" Rachel asked as she slipped into her coat.

"What? No," Corey scoffed.

Thayer arched a brow at her and cleared her throat theatrically. "I don't recall asking for your opinion."

She smiled sheepishly. "Sorry, babe. Your body, your rules."

Thayer reached for her hand to take the sting out of her admonishment. "We really need to get going."

"Me too, please." Rachel bounced up and down on her toes and looked at them imploringly.

Corey shook her head. "No, dude."

"No, wait, Corey." Thayer placed a hand on her arm. "Maybe this is a good idea to have something besides shenanigans to lead with when we introduce ourselves."

"Shenanigans?" asked Rachel. "Do I even want to know what you two have gotten yourselves into now?"

"No," they answered in unison.

CHAPTER FOURTEEN

The church was small compared to others in the city, and Corey took the half-dozen stone steps leading up to large oak double doors two at a time. Rachel was right behind her. The entire building was red brick with gorgeous stained-glass windows along both sides.

Rachel raised her hand and hesitated. "Do we knock?"

"How the hell should I know?"

"Isn't it a house?"

"Yeah, God's house."

"Have you two never been in a church before?" Thayer joined them in front of the door and switched her medical kit to her other hand. She pulled the door open. "Honestly, the things we still have to learn about each other."

"I hear music." Corey grinned at the sound of electric guitar and drums. "It's your siren song."

They stepped into a well-lit space with faux-marble tile. There was a half wall in front of them opening into the brightly lit church.

"Oh, a foyer," Corey said and looked around to the left and right of the entryway. There was a staircase leading down on either side a few yards away.

"The narthex," Thayer said.

"The what?" Rachel asked.

"It's called the narthex." Thayer gestured to the space. "The area we're in."

"That's not a word," Corey said.

"It is. And it leads into the nave, where the congregation sits." Thayer gestured to different parts of the space and gave a quick verbal tour of the inside of the church from where they stood.

Corey pursed her lips. "How do you even know this?"

"Because I'm smart." Thayer gripped her hand, lacing their fingers together. "And because I went to church with Nana for years, Sunday school and all."

They stepped through and stood at the back, trying not to interrupt the obvious rehearsal. In front of the first row of pews was an entire band set up—drum kit, keyboard, guitars with stands and standing microphones. A woman was speaking to the three young men lined up with their instruments who were listening intently to her instructions. All three of the kids looked thin and rangy with shaggy skater hair and baggy clothes.

"Is your boy there?" Corey whispered.

"No."

Seeming to sense their presence the woman turned, looking them over for a moment before smiling warmly at them. "Welcome," she called in a clear voice. "If you don't mind we have one more run through and then I'll be right with you."

"Thank you." Thayer gestured to the pew to their right. "It's okay if we listen?"

"Please do. The acoustics at the back are best."

Thayer pulled Corey in with her and sat down with Rachel sliding in next to Corey.

Corey ran her hands across the seat, upholstered in a soft sage green fabric. "Not what I expected at all."

"It's clearly been redone and updated. I doubt this is what it looked like before. This is much more modern."

Corey nodded and looked around. The floors were all faux marble except for the aisles running down the length between the rows of pews which were carpeted in the same sage green. The pulpit and lectern on the left and right of the sanctuary were new maple with simple clean lines, not the old ornate designs that were probably characteristic of the original church. Except for the original stained-glass windows, it had all been redone.

"Ready?" The woman spoke loudly enough that Corey could just hear. "I know it's been a long day and this song takes on new meaning now. Last time and then we're done."

The young men nodded eagerly, hands poised at the ready as she stepped up to the microphone and they could see her clearly for the first time. She was not tall, maybe five-foot six or a bit shorter. She had a striking, shock-white streak through dark, wavy hair swept off her face and fastened somewhere behind. She began to sway, full hips moving with the slow haunting keyboard intro, her head turned to the young man playing, and she smiled encouragingly, her hands cupping the microphone.

"This is 'Better Days' by the Goo Goo Dolls." She began to sing low and sultry. The drums and guitar began and the tempo picked up.

"Wow," Corey breathed and nudged Thayer. The woman looked like Adele and sounded like Brandi Carlisle.

"She's incredible," Thayer agreed.

Corey kept an eye on Thayer while they watched. She was as at ease as she had seen her in a long time. "How did I not know you were religious?" she whispered.

Thayer swayed with the music slightly, her mouth curving into a small smile. "I think 'religious' might be overstating it, but church has played a large part in my life at times."

"What religion?"

Thayer's gaze flicked to her. "Raised Catholic, but my father was somewhat lapsed—except when it suited him."

Corey grunted. "I guess that explains his reaction when you came out."

"Hmm, yes, I suppose it does. In the summers with Nana I had been part of a very welcoming Episcopal church, so by the time I came out, I wasn't in danger of abandoning my faith entirely."

"But it's not a part of your life now?"

"Faith is very much a part of my life now—church not so much. Not since medical school, anyway. No time, or rather, I haven't made the time."

"I understand." Corey nodded, not sure she did and uncertain where to take the conversation next. She glanced at Rachel and bit down on her lip to keep from laughing out loud at the dopey look on Rachel's face. She put her arm around Thayer and gestured toward Rachel.

"Uh oh," Thayer whispered. "Is that what the kids mean by *heart eyes?*"

Nora Warren's eyes were closed as she sang the last verse, and when the light was right, it looked like she was crying. The space filled with her powerful voice and emotion and the band played out the song. At the last note she turned and beamed at the young men. They grinned back at her, eyes shining. "That was perfect guys. Just like that for the service."

Corey and Thayer clapped and Rachel actually stood and whistled along with her applause.

The woman gave them a wave and smile. "All right guys. We're done. You can head back to the house."

There was a quick group hug before the three of them unplugged instruments, replaced guitars on stands and covered the keyboard and drums. They grabbed coats and took off out a side door.

"Thank you," the woman said as she made her way down the aisle toward them. Her speaking voice was as rich and smooth as her singing. She brushed away tears and smiled. "Forgive me, I don't usually cry at my own rehearsals, but I'm having an emotional day."

"We're the ones who should be apologizing, just showing up here unannounced," Thayer said. "You have an incredible voice."

"I'm pleased you enjoyed it," she said without a trace of self-consciousness. "We're working on the music for the New Years' service. Although that particular song," she cleared her throat and swallowed hard, "may serve as an unexpected tribute." Her expression lightened and she extended her hand toward Thayer first. "I'm Nora Warren."

"Very pleased to meet you, Reverend Warren. I'm Thayer Reynolds."

"Nora, please." She turned to Corey. "Hi, welcome."

"Corey Curtis." Corey shook her hand. Her grip was warm and she took a moment to study her. She had fair skin with a smattering of freckles, white teeth with an endearing gap in the front. She was dressed casually in a long sweater dress with black leggings and knee-high boots covering an alluringly lush figure.

She turned to Rachel, her smile widening as she held out her hand. "You're Rachel Wiley."

"I know I'd remember if we'd met." Rachel shook her hand, her eyes widening slightly when Nora Warren's other hand covered their clasped ones in an intimate gesture before releasing her.

"I've been to a couple of your charity concerts and Kelly was speaking of you just the other day. It seems we have similar interests and it's occurred to me that perhaps we should be collaborating on some of the work we do for the community."

"I, uh, yes, that's great, I mean..." Rachel stammered and trailed off.

Nora smiled. "I've wanted to introduce myself but you always seem to have a lot of people vying for your time."

She straightened in an apparent effort to pull herself together. "I would have made time for you."

Corey smothered a laugh and Thayer nudged her in the ribs.

Nora looked between the three of them. "What can I do for you, ladies?"

"Well, actually, that's why we're here: Rachel's work," Thayer said. "Well, that's one reason anyway."

"Oh? What's the other?"

Thayer cleared her throat and Corey gave her a nod to continue. "I'm an ED physician at JCMH and on Christmas Eve one of my patients gave me your card. I believe he may live at AllWays House."

Nora's smile faltered. "Is something wrong?"

"No, not at all. But I have reason to believe he may not have had an opportunity to fill a prescription I gave him. I wanted to check on him and provide him with the medicine if he needs it."

Nora's eyes narrowed. "A house call?"

"I know it's unusual, but even in the short time we interacted I came to care about him and I want to make sure he's okay," Thayer said truthfully, if not completely.

Nora appeared to take this at face value and nodded knowingly. "You've been very professional in not revealing his name, but I know to whom you refer. Were it anyone else, I may be skeptical, but Jeremy is a rare soul and his beauty touches just about everyone he meets. He's in the band, too, but hasn't been well, as you know."

"Do you think he would see me?" Thayer asked.

"We can ask. Give me a few minutes to lock up here and I'll walk you back to the house."

CHAPTER FIFTEEN

As soon as Nora Warren disappeared, Rachel erupted. "Holy shit, you guys, Nora Warren is amazing."

"She does have a fabulous voice," Thayer agreed. "She's obviously had a great deal of training."

Corey smirked. "I don't think that's the part Rachel was commenting on."

"Shut up, dude, I don't need your help."

"Says the woman who led with 'I would have made time for you.'" Corey mimicked her comically. A moment later the lights went out. "See? Even God thinks your game sucks."

"Shut it. I mean it, Corey. Don't fuck this up. This is business."

"Funny business," Corey muttered. "Show a little fucking restraint."

"Are you kidding me right now?" Rachel hissed. "You even admitted you had zero fucking chill when it came to Thayer and—"

"Will you two stop being ridiculous?" Thayer cut them off.

"Who's being ridiculous?" Nora asked as she appeared with her coat on from a door leading behind the sanctuary.

"These two." Thayer wagged a finger between Corey and Rachel. "They squabble like siblings and it's entirely possible this is the first time they've been in a church. Apparently, they are unsure how to behave."

"Still expecting the roof to catch on fire?" Nora's smile flashed in the darkness. "Don't worry. We hose it down once a month just for occasions like this. Even heathens are welcome here."

Thayer laughed out loud. "It's like you've met them before."

They exited out the side door and Nora locked it behind them. A few steps lead to a winding walkway lit with solar lights that took them farther onto the church property toward a well-appointed, two-story colonial in the same red brick as the church.

"This was the rectory but has been repurposed for AllWays House," Nora explained.

"You didn't want to use it?" Thayer asked.

"There would be so much wasted space if it were just me rattling around in there."

"That's cool of you," Corey said.

"Well, it wasn't just altruistic on my part. Can you imagine how much time to yourself you'd *never* get if you lived where you worked?" She led them up the front porch and knocked.

"Aren't you the director?" Corey asked, unsure why they weren't just walking in.

"Yes, but I try to give the guys their autonomy and privacy. Jeremy is the onsite resident manager. It helps to build trust and confidence. I do have a key, of course, but knocking works just as well."

"Is it only boys?" Thayer asked.

"It is at the moment but we do have room available for young women. We just get more young men. They're more likely to have a hard time at home and more likely to run away and find themselves at risk."

The door opened to one of the young men from the band whose shaggy bangs completely hid his eyes. "Hey, Nora, what's up?"

"Declan, these are some friends of mine, Corey, Rachel and Thayer. They'd like to see the house and speak with me. Do you mind if we come in for a bit?"

Declan paused for a moment, presumably peering at them through his hair, then swung the door wide. "Trey's upstairs studying, Cole's on the phone with his sponsor and the rest of us are binging *Stranger Things* if you want to join."

"We'll stay out of your way and be in the kitchen." Nora led the way into the house.

"Sorry about the smell," Declan called over his shoulder. "Leo can't make popcorn for shit."

Nora laughed. "It's fine. Where's Jeremy?"

Declan poked his head back out of the room. "He was feeling like garbage and went to his room."

He disappeared back into the darkened family room with the flickering of the television lighting up several faces. They went toward the back of the house into a large kitchen with formica counters, lots of storage space, and large, stainless-steel appliances.

"Please, have a seat." Nora gestured to the kitchen table with room for six and opened a cabinet. "Can I interest any of you in coffee? I still have a few hours of work to get to tonight and I could use a jolt."

"Coffee, yes," Rachel said. "My favorite."

Nora smiled shyly. "I love my coffee but I'm embarrassed to admit I'm not very discerning and we only have generic, or there may be some Dunkin' but that usually goes first."

"Oh, no, don't worry about that." Rachel waved carelessly. "I make a mean americano but I'm not actually a coffee snob."

Corey's eyes widened incredulously at Rachel but she didn't comment.

"Shut up," Rachel mouthed at her.

"Don't worry, Thayer, I didn't forget about you." Nora set the coffee maker on. "I'll just go let Jeremy know you're here."

"Thank you, Nora, I really appreciate this." She adjusted her medical kit higher on her shoulder.

"Dr. Reynolds." Jeremy stood in the doorway with Nora less than a minute later looking pale with watery, red-rimmed eyes. "What are you doing here?"

Thayer gave him a smile. "Call me Thayer. I was worried about you, and I was hoping you'd let me check on you. Privately."

"Oh, um, yeah, sure," he said uncertainly and coughed into his elbow. "If you don't mind coming to my room, I guess."

"I don't mind. I have a very good immune system."

The coffeemaker burbled its completion and Nora headed over to the cabinet to get down mugs. "Corey?"

"Sure, thanks." Corey sat back and slung an arm over the back of the chair watching Rachel with no small amount of humor and interest.

"You have an incredible voice, Nora," Rachel began. "Have you, you know, performed professionally?"

"Thank you, and yes, in a manner of sorts." She joined them at the table with coffee, milk and sugar. "I have a degree in Musical Theater from Syracuse; yes, that's a thing, much to my parents' dismay. Then I was fortunate to be accepted to Manhattan School of Music for a Master's. I performed in school, but not for money."

"That's so cool," Rachel said. "Then what?"

"Then I stayed in the city waiting to be discovered and become famous on Broadway."

"Did you?"

"What? You haven't heard of me? No, you're more famous than I am. I've seen your cover of JC Magazine."

Rachel blushed furiously. "Oh, that was not that big a deal."

"I disagree," Nora said. "Achieving your dreams is a very big deal."

If possible, Rachel reddened further, and as funny as it was watching her flounder when she was usually so smooth Corey took pity on her and went in for the rescue. "So, how did you end up here? I mean in the church as a…"

"Minister?"

"Yeah, sorry." Corey winced.

"Kelly didn't tell you? I was struck by lightning." She gestured to her hair.

"Holy shit!" Rachel blurted.

Corey sat forward in her chair. "Really?"

Nora laughed. "No, not really. It's called a mallen streak. It's hereditary. You two are too easy. It's just a joke I tell when people ask about my hair or profession."

Corey snorted. "Getting struck by lightning is the kinda thing that'd probably happen to either one of us, so it's not out of our way to believe something like that."

"Yeah," Rachel agreed. "Random unfortunate events are sort of our thing—especially lately."

Nora's gaze flicked between them. "I hope this isn't one such unfortunate event."

"No way," Rachel said. "So, how *did* you get into, um…"

"The ministry? You really want to know?"

"I do. Is that okay?"

Nora sat back with her cup of coffee. "Well, the short answer, as with many people who are fortunate enough to find their passion and do what they love, is that it's a calling. For me a call to serve. And I don't just mean to serve God, but to serve people. I didn't necessarily recognize it for what it was right off. I was gifted with vocal talent and I used that to bring people together. I sang at weddings and funerals and performed in many church choirs and fundraisers. I'd like to think I helped bring joy or comfort or whatever people needed from the encounter. It was very satisfying but never enough. Too often in our world, especially now, religion is weaponized and divisive and it breaks my heart. I wanted to serve a community in a way that brings people, no matter their faith, back together. I didn't know right away that when I decided to go to seminary I would become a minister, but in addition to my internal call, there were external forces very much in favor of this path for me and I followed."

"So, how did you end up in Jackson City?" Rachel asked.

"Once you are a servant of God you go where God says, or rather, the church sends you. In my case, I'm a hometown girl. This church was in dire need of major repairs—a new roof, plumbing, electrical and some foundation work—and the Catholic diocese didn't want to invest the money in the small congregation when most of their community was attending the cathedral. The UU church swept in and bought the property, made the repairs and updates and I fought very hard to be posted here."

Rachel eyed her. "Did you go to JC High?"

"I did. A few years before your time, I'd wager."

Rachel frowned. "Not too many."

"Hmm." A smile played at Nora's lips and she switched her attention from Rachel to Corey. "So, Corey, I know what Rachel does, how do you put toilet paper on the table?"

"I'm the Autopsy Services Coordinator at JCMH."

Nora straightened. "Autopsy? As in you perform them?"

"That's correct. It's kind of a conversation killer. No pun intended."

Her expression clouded for a brief moment before her gaze focused on Corey again. "That's fascinating."

Rachel snorted a laugh. "Most people think that and ask to hear about a case and then Corey gets overly generous with the gory details."

"It's not really as seen on television," Corey said.

"Tell me something anyway," Nora said, eyes sparkling with interest.

"Tell her about the case you and Thayer got together over," Rachel suggested.

"Yes, tell me. Sparing the gory details."

Jeremy sat on the edge of his bed. "Do you need me to, like, take my shirt off or something?"

"No." Thayer gestured to the spot next to him. "May I?"

"Yeah, yes." He scooted over toward the head of the bed and watched her nervously.

"What I need you to do is listen to me for a minute." Thayer dug in her bag and pulled out an inhaler. "This is a sample from the hospital. I know you didn't fill the prescription I gave you."

"I, uh, I didn't…" He flushed red. "How could you possibly know that?"

Thayer pulled Collier's card from her pocket. "You need to call Sergeant Jim Collier as soon as possible."

"The cops?" He took the card with a shaky hand and paled visibly. "Am I in trouble?"

"No, Jeremy." Thayer placed a comforting hand on his arm. "You're not in any trouble. But I do believe you got into trouble after you left the hospital on Christmas Eve and the police need to speak with you."

"I didn't." His voice cracked. "I didn't do anything wrong, Thayer. It was those…fucking assholes."

"Jeremy, stop. I can't know the details. I'm sorry, and I can't tell you how I know what I do. Jim Collier is a friend of mine and you can trust him."

"Yeah, okay." He bobbed his head, his voice wavering.

"You know what? You must know Kelly Warren, right? Nora's brother?"

His eyes brightened, color flooding his cheeks. "Kelly, yeah."

"I totally agree. He is very good looking. He works with Sergeant Collier and will probably be there to speak with you as well, okay?"

He stared at the card. "Does Nora know?"

"I didn't tell her anything."

"Okay. Do you think it would be all right if I called in the morning?"

Thayer covered his hand with her own. "I think that would be fine. Promise me?"

"I'll do it. I promise."

"Oh, my, word. That was you?" Nora gasped and covered her mouth with a hand in shock when Corey finished telling her about the details of her accident at the construction site, her recovery and reconnection with Thayer. "I thought your names sounded familiar. That's why you wear the glasses now, because of the headaches?"

"Yes." Corey adjusted them. "The headaches are far less frequent now, but when they happen, they still knock me on my ass for a day or so."

"Have you heard of Saint Teresa of Avila?"

Corey pulled the medallion from beneath her collar. "It was a gift from a friend."

"A good friend." She looked up right as Thayer came back into the kitchen. "Thayer, you two have had quite the adventurous romance."

"I'd say it's more like *misadventurous*." Thayer dropped into a chair next to Corey and placed a hand on her leg, smiling suspiciously. "Trying to curry favor with the woman upstairs?"

"Who, me? Please."

"Is everything okay with Jeremy?" Nora asked.

"He's going to be just fine. No need to worry." She glanced at Rachel. "Was Nora able to help you out with the music for the party?"

"Oh, uh, we didn't talk about that. It's not important."

Nora eyed Rachel expectantly. "What's not?"

Corey scowled at her. "Not important? It's why you're here. You were totally freaking out."

"Really. It's not a big deal."

"If you tell me what it is you need, Rachel, I'd be happy to help any way I can. It's what I do," Nora said.

"Thank you." Rachel reddened again and scraped back hard in her chair. "I've taken up enough of your time. You said you have more work to do and I should be getting back to help close up the shop." She whipped her coat back on and offered a weak smile. "It was really nice to meet you, Nora. You guys don't have to leave; I'll just grab an Uber."

She was out the front door before anyone else stood and Corey and Thayer shared a bewildered look.

"Is that normal?" Nora appeared more bemused than offended at Rachel's abrupt departure.

"I don't know what that was." Corey smiled apologetically. "All she wanted to do was ask you if—"

"Corey," Thayer interrupted, gently. "If Rachel has changed her mind, we should stay out of her business."

"Fine. Whatever. She's probably just out front, so we should go. Really great to meet you, Nora. Maybe we'll see you again soon."

"From your lips to God's ears."

CHAPTER SIXTEEN

"What was up with Rachel in there?" Thayer asked when they got in the car after walking the block looking for her for a few minutes. Rachel was long gone.

"Your guess is as good as mine. I'm going to go by the shop in the morning and worm it out of her."

"That sounds like a good idea."

"Are you okay?" Corey slid her hand over Thayer's leg.

"I'm fine." Thayer removed her hand. "Two hands on the wheel, please. It's dark and icy."

"Yes, ma'am."

"You can use both hands for something else when we get home," Thayer said with a sweet smile.

"Yes, ma'am," Corey replied enthusiastically. "How did everything go with Jeremy?"

"As well as expected, I guess. He's anxious, but I assured him as best I could that's he's not in trouble and that Jim is trustworthy. He already knows Kelly, so I think it should be fine. He's going to call Jim in the morning."

"And how do you feel about it all?"

Thayer inhaled, deeply. "Confident that I handled a difficult situation the best way that I could to preserve my professional and ethical obligations and be true to my moral ones at the same time."

"So, you gave it zero thought is what you're saying?"

Thayer laughed and turned in her seat, running her hand up the inside of Corey's leg and making her jump. "You make me laugh."

"I thought you wanted me focus on the road, woman."

"Are you hungry?" Thayer shed her winter clothes while Corey let Charlie out of the kitchen and played on the floor with her.

"Famished." She stood and pulled her headlamp from the hook. "Gotta take the little miss for a run, though."

"Right now?" Thayer looked out the back windows. Despite it being just eight, the flurries started to come down in the very dark night.

Corey pointed toward the living room at one of Thayer's sneakers with a hole chewed through the sole.

"Aw, why is it always *my* shoes?" She snatched the sneaker off the floor and looked around for any other evidence of Charlie's bad behavior. "Did you do this?" She held the shoe out to the puppy who promptly sat politely, tail thumping at Thayer's attention.

"She's shameless. Between the two of you I can never have nice things. Wait, how did she get out? The gate was closed, right?"

Corey shrugged. "I don't know. Over the top maybe?"

"She climbed the gate, chewed my shoe in the living room, and then went back over the gate to where she's supposed to be so we would't notice?"

"What's your suggestion?" Corey grimaced at the absurdity of it.

Thayer sighed and threw her shoe in the trash. "I think we should get a crate."

"Shh, no." Corey covered the dog's ears. "We're not putting her in a cage."

"Well, something is going to change." Thayer crossed her arms.

Charlie barked and wriggled back and forth between them. Corey ruffled her ears. "It's okay, Charlie, Mom and Mommy are just talking. It's not you."

Thayer snorted a laugh. "It *is* her and I better not be 'mommy.' I hate that."

"I'll take her out for longer in the morning," she said. "And when I can I'll come back during the day."

"*You're* going to get up earlier?"

"Whoa, now, don't get crazy. I'll just go in later. We can't carpool next week, anyway."

"Fine." Thayer stripped out of her clothes. "I'm going to grab a shower, check in with Nana, and fix us something to eat."

Corey flung the door open, letting in a blast of cold air. "Come on, Charlie, let's go." The puppy bounded across the porch and into the snow.

When she came back in an hour later, the lights were dim. She could hear the crackling of the fire and the house smelled amazing. "Is that bacon?"

Thayer responded from the great room. "I made you a BLT. I didn't have any more energy than that."

Corey fed and watered Charlie and slipped her a piece of bacon before closing the gate to the kitchen. "Sorry, girl, there can be only one," she whispered. "I'll come back for you later."

Thayer was in front of the fire lounging against the pillows on the bearskin rug. She was dressed in yoga pants and a tank top with a very large glass of wine in one hand, resting against her stomach.

"Did you eat already?" Corey joined her with a beer and her sandwich, sitting cross legged next to her.

"Yes, while I was talking to Nana."

"What's new in Lil's world? Did she have a nice Christmas?"

"She called my mother."

Corey paused, the sandwich in front of her mouth. "Oh? How did that go?"

Thayer took a long sip from her wine. "Good, she says."

"Why don't you sound happy about it? It's what you wanted, right? Seems like everything is swinging back your way."

"Funny you should phrase it like that. I was just thinking the pendulum may have swung back too far in the other direction."

"What do you mean?"

"I mean in the car an hour ago I just went on about how I handled everything to suit *me* and *my* needs. I was feeling out of control and I took control of the things I could. Now I just feel like I've imposed my will on people—Nana, Jim, Jeremy, you—without making room for the feelings of anyone else. I didn't consider what anyone else wanted or needed."

Corey sucked on her beer for a moment. "Sorry, babe, but I think you're giving yourself too much credit."

"Thanks."

"I mean, your opinion matters to people and they respect what you think, but I sincerely doubt you influenced anyone to do anything they didn't want to do."

"Maybe."

"Not *maybe*. When's the last time you got Lil to do something she didn't want to do?"

Thayer smiled grimly. "Three nevers ago."

"That's what I thought. And seriously, if Collier had really wanted for things to play out differently with that body, he would have imposed *his* will. I'm actually surprised at how quietly he backed down over that. He likes you way more than he likes me."

"Did you talk to him about it?"

"Nope. Haven't seen or heard from him since this morning. He was pretty busy with the...shooting victim."

"Hmm, right. He'll probably be around first thing after he speaks with Jeremy."

"Probably." Corey finished her beer and moved the empty bottle and Thayer's wine glass to the coffee table. "In the meantime, since you're feeling like such a bully, how about I take you down a peg?" She swung her leg over Thayer's hips and straddled her.

"You think you can?" Thayer's smile was teasing. "Rumor has it I'm pretty full of myself."

Corey grazed her fingertips down Thayer's bare arms and threaded their fingers together. "I think I can put you in your place." She raised Thayer's hands and kissed the back of each one before leaning forward, stretching her arms above her head and pinning her to the floor.

"Mmm." Thayer murmured, her body tightening beneath Corey, her hips rising against her.

Corey shifted, slipping her leg between Thayer's thinly clad thighs and rocking into her. "I'm leading this."

Thayer sighed and stilled. "You're going to mess around, aren't you?" she asked.

"Yes." Corey stopped whatever she was going to say next by covering Thayer's mouth with her own. Thayer's soft moan sent a streak of heat straight between her legs. Corey slid her hands down Thayer's arms and kneaded her breasts through her tank. "Leave your arms there."

Thayer arched, her body responding intensely to Corey's skillful ministrations when she bit at her nipples, hardening them though her tank. She gasped, her fingers curling around the base of the coffee table, just within her reach.

Corey teased her breasts for another moment before having enough of the fabric between them. She lifted Thayer's tank over her head and flung it away. She scooted down, pulling at the waistband of her pants and Thayer lifted her hips, allowing her to pull them off easily.

Corey straddled her again and made no move to take off her own clothes. She studied Thayer, naked beneath her, lips parted and chest rising and falling rapidly with the arousal that danced in her fire-lit golden eyes. "Feeling humbled yet?"

"Humility—is that what this feeling is?"

Corey smoothed her hands over Thayer's belly and around her breasts in a circular motion. "Just imagine, in less than two weeks I could be applying sunscreen just like this."

Thayer smiled lazily, her hips twitching with every pass of her hands across her chest. "To my breasts?"

"Why not?"

"For one thing, I have no intention of being topless outside. For the other…" She gazed down. "These are all the spots I can reach on my own."

Corey grinned and slipped a hand between her legs. "You can reach this spot on your own, too, but isn't it nicer when I reach it for you?"

Thayer sucked in a sharp breath at the touch. "Take your clothes off."

"No." Corey lowered herself again, this time using tongue and teeth along Thayer's neck and clavicle. Moving tantalizingly slowly, she circled her pointed nipples with the tip of her tongue and grazed the sides of her breasts with her fingers.

Thayer wriggled beneath her. "Oh, hell."

"Can you come from just breast stimulation?" Corey asked, lifting her mouth from around a nipple.

"What? No. I don't know."

"I'm gonna try." Corey went back to what she was doing—lavishing one nipple with her tongue, sucking it into her mouth hard and rolling the other between her fingertips.

"Oh, god, what are you…" Thayer's words trailed off on a shuddering gasp of pleasure.

Corey sucked and nibbled, kneading her breasts endlessly until Thayer was a writhing, panting, sweaty mess beneath her. "Are you close?" she mumbled, pulling on a nipple with her teeth.

"Not…close…enough," she panted, arching and twisting under her.

"I need more time."

"You need…to move down…or I'm…gonna scream."

"Oh, all right." Corey grinned wickedly, meeting her glazed, hooded eyes while she slid her right hand down between Thayer's legs. "But you're gonna scream anyway."

Thayer sucked in a breath and froze when Corey's fingertips teased her center before slipping inside, eliciting a long, desperate groan from deep within.

"Like that?" Corey asked, curling her fingers, pressing against her walls, feeling Thayer's muscles contract tight around her hand.

"More."

Corey's thumb circled her swollen clit, adding pressure and increasing the speed of her strokes. "Close now?"

Thayer's mouth dropped open, her hips bucking against Corey's hand as her orgasm exploded through her in a powerful climax. She cried out in her release and Charlie howled from the kitchen along with her.

CHAPTER SEVENTEEN

Corey marched directly to the back of Rachel's shop at nine the next morning, dodging the usual weekday morning crowds. It was snowing again and Thayer had made a strong case for Corey not driving her truck. She had dropped Thayer off for her shift at eight and swung by the morgue to take the body's temperature, check in with Webster, and make sure there were no pending cases before heading out again to find out why Rachel hadn't answered any of her texts.

The back corner of the cafe was Rachel's preferred office space as opposed to the actual private office which she had converted to a breakroom for the staff. It looked like someone dropped a paperwork bomb on the table. Rachel was on the phone hunched over her laptop and gesticulating wildly at the screen.

Corey dropped into a chair to wait. Lainey must have seen her come in and brought her a cup of coffee. "Thanks, Lainey." She gestured to Rachel who hadn't even acknowledged her. "What's her deal?"

"Dunno. She's been like this since she came back last night."

"Insane?"

"Your problem. We're slammed."

"Fine, thank you. I'll be here," Rachel barked into the phone before stabbing it off. She looked up, eyes narrowing at Corey. "*What's* your problem?"

Corey slurped her coffee. "*You*, apparently."

"What does that mean?" Rachel peered around the table at the three partially empty mugs. She chose the nearest one and took a sip. Grimacing at the taste she pushed it away.

"Why were you so weird last night? Just taking off like that was kinda rude—even for you."

Rachel opened her mouth like she was about to fire back a barb before her jaw clicked shut and she visibly deflated, dropping her head into her hands. "I was a total dick, wasn't I?"

Corey smiled sympathetically. "Partial, maybe, not total. What the hell happened?"

She muttered unintelligibly into her hands.

"What?"

"Feelings." She raised her head, dragging her hands through her hair on the way making it stick up everywhere. "I think I maybe started to have feelings and I panicked."

"Feelings. Like, grown up feelings?"

"Yes."

"Like more than just in your pants feelings?"

"Yeah."

"How can you possibly have *feelings* for a woman you just met?"

Rachel scowled at her. "Really, dude? *You're* asking me that?"

"Okay, well—"

"Well, what? I looked at this woman and it was like she was lit from within and I felt like Carol Ann with this crazy pull and this voice inside my head going 'Rachel, go into the light.'"

Corey blinked at her for a moment before throwing her head back in laughter. "Rach, there's so many things wrong with comparing the lovely minister to a poltergeist I don't even know where to start."

"You know what I mean. She has, like, her own psychic soundtrack and every time I look at her I hear, 'She Keeps Me Warm' and I feel like I've been wrapped in a snuggie."

"Am I interrupting?"

Corey jumped and Rachel stood so fast her chair tipped over when they saw Nora Warren standing at their table.

"Holy shit." Rachel gaped at her.

Nora smiled apologetically. "It appears I am. I'm sorry. I'll go."

Rachel snapped out of her daze. "What? No, *I'm* sorry. That was terrible. I don't usually greet people like that."

Corey pushed her chair back. "You know what? I'll go."

"No," Rachel and Nora both said at the same time.

Rachel looked at Corey wild eyed. "Please, stay."

"You don't have to leave, Corey," Nora said. "I just wanted to make sure Rachel was okay after she left so fast. And I admit, after all the mystery, I'm incredibly intrigued by whatever it is you wanted, but then didn't want to ask me."

Corey pulled out the other chair, gesturing for Nora to join them. Rachel remained standing until she caught Lainey's attention. With an elaborate series of hand gestures, she apparently asked for coffee and snacks for them, as a moment later a carafe of coffee and a tray of pastries appeared.

Nora poured herself a cup and added milk and sugar. Corey freshened up her coffee and grabbed a cheese biscuit and glanced at Nora out of the corner of her eye. She was adorable in black, calf-high winter boots over well-fitting jeans, beige cowl neck sweater with a pale blue puffer vest over it. Her hair was piled atop her head in a messy bun shot with white from the mallen streak.

Nora sipped her coffee, savoring it. "Oh, dear, I'm going to get spoiled. This is delicious. What's it called?"

"It's just the house blend," Rachel said.

"It's not *just* anything. It's rich and wonderful and has character."

Even Corey's heart gave a little lurch with how much joy Nora Warren could take from a simple cup of coffee, how in the moment she seemed to be.

Nora cradled her mug to her chest in two hands and sat back to cross her legs. "Now, are you going to tell me what that was about last night? What did you come to ask me?"

"We are SOL, Rachel," Lainey announced as she rushed over to the table waving her hands. "Sorry to interrupt. Womenstruation is a no go. They're playing at First Night."

Rachel sighed. "Okay. It was a long shot. Did you try the Byrne Trio?"

"Yep."

"Cam Delmar?"

"Yes. And before you keep going, I have contacted everyone who has played here. There is no one to play for New Year's," Lainey said with finality.

"You need a band," Nora said. "That's why you came to me?"

"I came to see if you could suggest someone. I didn't even know you had your own until last night."

"So, why didn't you ask me?"

"Yeah, why?" Corey said.

"Because…" Rachel shrugged helplessly. "I heard you sing and you were incredible and then I heard you speak and you're incredible. I suspected you would say yes and I didn't want you to feel like I was taking advantage of you. Having just met you and all."

Nora pursed her lips nodding. "That's very noble of you. What is the band needed for?"

"My New Year's Eve party."

"And who's going to be attending?"

"Uh, well, friends and business associates, members of the city council, Women's Business Association, and Chamber of Commerce mostly. Oh, and the partners at Tagliotti, Mancini and Castiglione—the law firm upstairs."

"The mob," Corey mumbled.

"Jesus, dude. Enough with that. They are not the fucking mob, and if they were do you really think we should be speaking openly about it within earshot? Sorry. Ignore her—and my language."

"Hmm." Nora took a long sip of her coffee. "So, what you're saying is whoever plays for your party will have the opportunity to hobnob with festively drunk, prominent members of the city?"

"Well, yes, I suppose that's true. I mean, that's why I'm throwing it, sort of. Laying some groundwork for expanding."

"So, ask me." Nora set her mug on the table and leaned forward, hands clasped around her knee.

Rachel's gaze darted to Corey who offered her what she hoped was an encouraging nod. Rachel smiled hesitantly. "Hey, Nora, I know we just met but would you and the fellas from AllWays House be interested in playing my New Year's Eve party?"

"What's it pay?" she asked.

"Oh, um, two grand?" Rachel suggested hesitantly.

"In a check made out to AllWays House?"

Rachel's brows rose hopefully. "Is that a yes?"

"May the rest of the residents come if they want? They won't be drinking, of course."

"Yeah, absolutely."

"Yes, then. What time would you like us here?"

"The party starts at nine, music from ten to one.

"We'll be here at eight to set up, rehearse, and get used to the space. Then we can mingle before we play. Does that work?"

"That works."

Nora grew thoughtful a moment. "Was Marcus Bright going to be at the party?"

Rachel winced. "He was, I think. God, that sucks about what happened. Did you know him?"

Nora's expression clouded. "I did. He wasn't a member of the congregation, but his wife, Lisa, and their children have been active in my church for a number of years. It's been..." Her voice wavered. "It's been a rough couple of days."

Corey sat up straight, her gaze flicking to Rachel who looked horrified. "I'm so sorry. We had no idea you were...And we just showed up last night."

"Oh, no." Nora placed a hand on her arm. "Please, don't worry about that. It's been nice to think about something else and meeting you all has been…" Her attention turned back to Rachel. "Has been a real blessing. Certainly, I'm thankful for the opportunity to play for you and for some of the people that were close to Marcus if they're going to be attending."

"I've never met him, but I know he was very highly regarded," Rachel said.

"Do you have any objections if I mentioned him and did a song in his honor?"

"I think that would be amazing, and I'm sure it would be appreciated."

"Okay, I'll see you in a few days. Is it all right to call you here if I have any questions?"

"Of course." Rachel beamed at her. "I don't know what to say."

"Say thank you."

"Thank you."

"You're most welcome."

They were both quiet as they watched Nora Warren thread her way through the morning crowds on her way to the door. Corey laughed softly when she actually stopped to pick up the tiny vase from an empty high-top table and smell the small cutting of purple stock that Rachel insisted ornament every table, even in winter.

"So, what do you think?" Rachel asked after Nora left.

Corey snorted. "I think you're punching above your weight class."

"Says the skid who's shacking up the with a gorgeous lady doctor."

"A priest, Rachel, really?"

"A minister."

"What's the difference?"

"I have no idea."

Corey spun her empty mug around on the table. "You know I'm just kidding around, right?"

"Yeah, I know, but you're right. I get the feeling she thinks I'm just some young punk anyway."

"No, I'm not right. Not even remotely. What is she, thirty-six? She's not even ten years older than you. She's my age-ish and that didn't stop us from giving it a try back in the day."

"Because we were horny and desperate and neither one of us had standards then."

"True. We were really scraping the bottom of the barrel that night."

"I think you mean bottom of the bottle." Rachel laughed with her for a moment before turning serious again. "So, for real, what do you think?"

"I think what you have built here is absolutely amazing." Corey swept her arm around the bustling coffee house. "And—"

"Did you know I'm going to be in JC magazine's top thirty under thirty issue?"

"Really? That's great! Now, shut the hell up. I'm trying to be profound."

"Sorry. Carry on."

"Damn it, now I don't remember what I was going to say, but the bottom line is, I think the only thing that could make all of this better is someone to share it with. Someone real, not just one of your flings, as fun as those probably are. You're making a real difference here and maybe it's time to consider taking on a partner, and I don't mean business partner. Someone who shares your vision, you know?"

"You make it sound so easy."

"Yeah, well, I don't mean to 'cause it's not. Even when Thayer and I both wanted it, I managed to fuck it up."

Rachel groaned. "I kinda think I'm doing a pretty good job of that already."

"Rach, no. She showed up here this morning to check on you. She practically swooned over your coffee and agreed to play your party."

"For money."

"Did you expect her to do it for free? You were going to pay those other fools, weren't you? And you were the one who was weird about not taking advantage of her. She was respecting that in the chillest possible way."

"Okay, so now what?"

"What is it you told me when I gushed over Thayer at the beginning? You do you and maybe soon you'll be doing Reverend—"

"Nope. No. Aboslutely not. She's a woman of the cloth. We do not discuss her like that."

CHAPTER EIGHTEEN

Corey spent the day doing paperwork to release Marcus Bright to the funeral home and taking time to untorque the frozen body. It had warmed up to thirty-two degrees and she could now, with effort, unbend the limbs and stretch him out, which would aid in the final day of thawing. She discussed the case with Webster and scheduled the autopsy for late morning the following day.

She hung by the morgue, expecting Collier to storm in any moment with more information on the body after having spoken to Jeremy Landis, but she didn't hear a word from him. She tried calling him once, but when it went straight to voice mail, she didn't leave a message. Somewhat at a loss as to what to do next, she debated tracking down Thayer but decided it was best not to worry her while she was at work. They could talk about it later when Thayer picked her up from the gym.

After inadvertently filling the last six months with nonstop drama and action, she didn't quite know what to do with herself, her life having gone back to the uneventful it had been before she met Thayer.

She clicked her way through emails, deleting most before she even read them, deciding they didn't have anything to do with her. After that menial task was exhausted she browsed through the local news online, skimming through articles about Marcus Bright that now referred to his death as a suicide. There were smiling pictures of him with his family at community events interspersed with quotes from 'shocked and saddened' coworkers, neighbors and grief-stricken family.

The end of the article had one brief quote from lead investigator, Sergeant Jim Collier, about the completion of the investigation and heartfelt condolences from the people of Jackson City to the Bright family.

Corey closed down her computer figuring that's what was keeping Collier so busy. Rachel picked her up from the morgue so she could leave the car at the hospital for Thayer.

Corey struggled to press the bar back up on her last repetition and it wavered dangerously over her throat for an uncomfortably long time. "Rach..." she grunted.

Rachel's hands shot out and gripped the bar, taking the weight and racking it. "Sorry. You okay?"

Corey sat up on the bench and shook out her arms. "Where is your head at tonight?"

"What? Nowhere. I'm fine."

"Liar."

"Gah! I can't stop thinking about her."

"Who, Nora?" Corey mopped her face with a towel. "Oh, Christ."

"I'm enthralled. Enchanted. Bewitched."

"Ensorcelled?"

"Totally and completely. You know how you described how you felt right when you met Thayer? I thought you were out of your goddamn mind, but I think I feel like that."

Corey jumped to her feet and headed toward the locker room. "Well, let's go see her then. I'll be your wing woman."

Rachel looked alarmed and hurried after her. "What—now? I mean, I can't fucking creep her."

"Did she or did she not show up unannounced at your place of work this morning?"

"My place of work is a coffee shop and you don't typically need to call ahead."

"Yeah, well, she drove across town when she has a Starbuck's in walking distance," Corey argued as she stripped out of her clothes.

Rachel shook her head and yanked her locker open. "Jesus!" She yelped and jumped back as the small bags of ground coffee flew out at her. "Where the hell has Tara been anyway? She bugged me for weeks to bring in all the sample bags for her husband. I need her to show up so I can get rid of all this shit." She scooped all the bags off the floor and set them on the bench.

"Pretty sure she pushed a tiny human out of her vag a couple of weeks ago." Corey wrapped a towel around her and headed for the showers.

"Oh, yeah. I guess that's allowed."

"If only you knew someone else who liked coffee that you needed an excuse to bump into," Corey mused loudly over the sound of the running water from her stall.

"Is that a joke?" Rachel called back. "That's stupid."

"This is stupid," Rachel grumbled as they trudged up the walkway toward the entrance to the church.

"So you keep saying." It was not yet seven but fully dark out, cold and blustery. Whereas last night light shone through the stained-glass windows in the sanctuary, tonight there was only a feeble lamp illuminating the walkway. Corey was not surprised when she tugged on the iron ring handle of the large wood doors to find it locked.

"Oh, well." Rachel threw up her hands and started back down the walkway.

"Hold on." Corey grabbed her by the hood pulling her up short. "Let's try the house."

"Absolutely, not."

"Holy Jesus, woman, you are being ridiculous right now. It's not late at all. What could it hurt to knock and see if she's there?"

"It's rude to show up unannounced, and stop taking the Lord's name in vain."

Corey blinked at her. "What's wrong with you?"

Rachel huffed, her breath coming out in a plume on the cold night air. "Nothing, I'm fine. It's fine. Let's go." She started around the path that led to the house.

"Hey, ladies," Jeremy Landis greeted them when he opened the door. "You were here the other night with Thayer. I'm sorry I don't remember your names."

"Corey." She hooked a thumb at herself. "And this is Rachel. We were looking for Reverend Warren. Is she here by any chance?"

"Uh, no. But you didn't miss her by much. She was heading home early. Do you know where she lives?"

"Refresh our memory." Corey fought a smile and ignored Rachel's withering glare.

"It's just down two blocks on the same side of the street. I don't know the number but you can't miss it. It's a cute little carriage house between a dentist and insurance office, restored Victorians on each side. There's a high fence she keeps locked at night so I'll text her and let her know you're on your way over."

"That's not necessary," Rachel whined, but it was too late. The kid texted with blazing speed.

"She'll keep an eye out for you." He grinned at them both, his eyes narrowing slightly as he looked Rachel up and down slowly, his smile widening further. "I think she'll be happy to see you."

Rachel smiled nervously. "Um, okay. Yeah, thank you."

"Cool coat, by the way." He gestured to Rachel's three-quarter length, black peacoat with hood. "I found one just like it on consignment and I love it. Is yours wool?"

"Oh, yeah." Rachel held out her arm for him to feel. "It's hella warm."

"If you take the path back and take the fork to the left, it crosses the grounds through the grove of trees and comes out onto the street a block closer to Nora's place. It's cleared of snow but may be a little icy," he said.

"Thanks." Corey waved and headed back down the path. When they came to the fork, Rachel turned to the left toward the shortcut to the street. "What about your car?"

"Oh, right." She dug in her messenger bag and tossed her the keys. "Can you move it? I'm going to walk."

"Need to rehearse your lines?"

"Shut up." Rachel turned back to the path and Corey laughed the rest of the way back to the street.

She slid behind the wheel of Rachel's car and pulled out her phone. She already had a text from Thayer letting her know she got away early and was going home to let Charlie out and check on her shoes.

She called rather than texted, knowing Thayer wouldn't pick up a text, but could answer the phone hands free. "Hey, babe, don't go to the gym."

"I'm already on my way back to town. Where are you?"

Corey started the car and turned the heat up. "At the church giving Rachel a shove in the right direction."

"That direction being toward Nora Warren?"

"I do believe the woman could be Rachel's path to enlightenment." She kept her eye out for Rachel to emerge on the street. She didn't want to head down the road until she knew exactly where she was going so she didn't overshoot the place.

"I know how you like to play matchmaker, but you better be careful how much you interfere or you'll just piss her off."

"Yeah, I know. I think I've already crossed that line. I just want her to be happy."

"I know you do, sweetheart. Where am I picking you up?"

"I don't know the exact street number, but it's two blocks from the church. A carriage house behind a high fence on the same side of the street as the church. You'll see Rachel's car." Corey cleared the glass of the few flurries with the wipers as Rachel came through the trees that lined the church property.

She hit the sidewalk heading away from Corey. A few moments later four dark-clad figures stepped out onto the sidewalk behind Rachel and rushed toward her. Rachel, hunched against the wind with her hood up, gave no indication she knew they were there.

"The fuck?"

"Corey, what's wrong?"

"I think Rachel's in trouble. Bring your kit."

CHAPTER NINETEEN

"Rachel!" Corey yelled through the windshield when she saw the largest of the four take a swing at Rachel's head from behind. Her heart leapt into her throat when Rachel staggered under the blow and went down on one knee. Corey threw the car in drive and accelerated dangerously fast up the block. The back end whipped around on the slushy road as she watched three of them close in on Rachel, kicking her while she was down. The smallest of the group hung back, jumping up and down and punching the air.

Rachel did not stay down for long and Corey could clearly see one of the assailants staggering back clutching his balls and another bending double, holding his gut.

The car fishtailed and skidded to a stop with one tire up on the curb. She leaned on the horn and flashed the headlights. The largest of the three clubbed Rachel again in the side of her face, sending her to the ground. Rachel kicked out, sending her heel snapping into his knee and folding him over with a shriek of pain.

Corey threw the door open at the same time the gate to the property flew open and Nora burst out onto the sidewalk. "I've called the police!" she yelled at the stumbling forms limping away down the block.

"Burn in hell, murdering fucking faggot!" the smallest one screeched as they disappeared around the corner.

Corey dropped to her knees in the slush next to Rachel, who was already struggling to get up. "Shit, Rach." Corey could see drops of bright, red blood dripping into the snow beneath her hanging head as she pushed up onto all fours.

"Fuck." Rachel gurgled and spat a mouthful of blood into the snow.

"Dear, God," Nora said shakily. "Can you get her into the house?"

Corey wanted to give Rachel a chance to catch her breath but thought it wiser to get off the street in case those assholes decided to come back or had friends nearby. Nora, apparently, had a similar thought and collected Rachel's bag. She stood guard on the street while Corey got an arm around Rachel's waist and hauled her to her feet.

"Take it easy," Rachel groaned.

"Sorry. I'm sorry." She moved them through the gate and down the walkway to the front door standing open.

Corey eased Rachel onto the sofa in the front room of the small carriage house. She lifted Rachel's head gently to see her face. Her left eye was rapidly swelling shut, and a shallow, two-centimeter laceration beneath it oozed blood. She also had a split and bleeding lip and bruising along the left side of her jaw. "Fuckers."

"I'm all right," Rachel slurred and shifted, clearly uncomfortable.

"Here, Corey." Nora handed her a cool damp towel.

"Thank you." Corey wrapped Rachel's left hand around it and pressed it gently to the left side of her face. "Hold this, Rach."

"Should I call an ambulance?" Nora asked worriedly.

"No," Rachel said.

"Thayer's on her way. She'll know what to do."

A sharp knock at the door startled them all followed by a rattling of the doorknob. "That's Kelly." Nora unlocked the door.

Kelly Warren's muscular, uniformed body filled the doorway before enveloping his sister in his arms. "You all right, Nora?" he asked as he held her at arm's length and looked her over.

"I'm fine." She stepped aside and gestured to the sofa. "It's my friends."

Corey stood as Kelly stared at her in surprise and Collier slid his giant frame behind him inside the doorway of the small house. They all stared at each other.

"Oh, shit," Collier and Corey muttered simultaneously.

"Gettin' the band back together," Rachel mumbled.

Kelly jumped into the silence. "Nora, this is Sergeant Jim Collier. Sarge, my sister, Reverend Nora Warren."

"Thank you for getting here so quickly, Sergeant Collier."

"Glad we were so close."

"Room for one more?" Thayer squeezed her way between Collier and Kelly, seemingly unfazed by the scene as she headed over to the sofa, pausing only briefly to slide her glance over Corey. Apparently satisfied she was uninjured, she set her satchel down on the floor and perched on the sofa next to Rachel. "How are you feeling, Rachel?"

"Like I got my ass kicked by a bunch of homophobic mouth breathers." Blood trickled from her mouth as she spoke.

"Can someone get me a bowl, please, and another cloth?" Thayer said. She held the offered bowl beneath Rachel's chin. "Spit in here. Don't swallow it."

Rachel leaned forward slightly and spit a wad of blood into the bowl. Thayer eased her mouth open and pressed an edge of the cloth into the back of her mouth. "Bite down. You're going to want to see your dentist when some of the swelling goes down to make sure nothing is loose."

"I need to call a bus, Doc?" Collier asked from near the doorway.

"No," Rachel mumbled around the towel.

Thayer didn't answer as she shone a pen light into Rachel's eyes. "Did you lose consciousness at all?" Thayer nodded when Rachel shook her head and palpated Rachel's face around her left eye and jaw. "I don't feel any facial fractures. Where else do I need to look?"

Rachel shifted forward and wrapped her right arm around her waist to her left flank. "Kicked."

Thayer unbuttoned her coat and helped her out of it, trying not to jostle her. She moved to her left side and pulled up her shirt revealing the purpling, crescent-shaped bruise over her kidney.

"Motherfuckers," Corey growled and her entire body tensed with rage. Her first instinct was to hit the street running and go after them, though she knew they were long gone.

She met Collier's gaze when she looked toward the door and the fury in his eyes matched her own. Her intentions must have been clear as he pinned her with a warning look and shook his head slowly.

"All right." Thayer looked around the small house and directed her next comment to Nora. "Bathroom's that way, I assume?"

"First door on the left." Nora watched Rachel worriedly.

"You're going to pee for me, Rachel," Thayer stated in a way that left no room for negotiation as she stood and picked up her bag. "Any blood and we're going to the hospital, understand?"

Rachel nodded and let Thayer help her to her feet. "Fun, yeah."

"Doc?" Collier called and waited for Thayer to turn. "Photo documentation of all injuries, okay? Your phone is fine."

"Of course," Thayer said as they moved slowly down the hall.

The rest of them remained silent for a long moment as they disappeared into the bathroom.

"Nora, what happened?" Kelly asked, his face the same expression of concern and anger the rest of them wore to varying degrees.

Nora's eyes were bright with unshed tears. "I don't know."

"Curtis?" Collier looked her over. "Are you hurt?"

"No, I'm fine," she said tightly.

He gestured vaguely to his own head. "You feel okay?"

She released a slow breath and realized how tense she was. She worked to relax her shoulders and rolled her head to loosen the muscles in her neck. She was painfully tense but nothing worse. "Yeah, I'm good, thanks." She offered him a brief smile and touched her fingertips to her chest where her medallion rested beneath her shirt.

He nodded. "You want to walk us through it? We'll speak with Wiley when Doc is done with her."

She zipped up her coat. "We gotta walk back to the church."

Kelly turned to her sister. "We'll talk more when we get back."

"I'll make some coffee."

"Oh, yeah." Corey retrieved Rachel's messenger bag and dug around in it for the bags of coffee handing them over to her.

"What are these?"

"Coffee from Rachel's shop she thought you might like," Corey said, not bothering with pretense. It was all going to come out anyway. "It's why we came over. She wanted an excuse to see you again."

Nora took the bags without comment, but Corey saw the flicker of a smile across her lips and the flush of heat in her cheeks.

CHAPTER TWENTY

Collier's notebook was out and he wrote furiously while Corey walked them back through their steps—where they parked, where they walked, why they were there. She didn't hold back. Rachel had been hurt and she didn't think it was random. She had a sickening feeling it was connected to the shelter, maybe to the frozen body, and maybe even to Nora Warren. Whatever was going on needed to be discovered.

When they walked around the church to the house, Corey stopped some distance from the front door and hoped no one inside saw them standing there. She knew the truth was all going to come out, but she wasn't sure if she should be the one to reveal it. "We came around to see if she was at the house."

"What's at the house?" Collier asked without looking up.

Corey paused long enough to raise his suspicions and he looked up from his notebook.

"It's a shelter for queer youth," Kelly said. "Runaways, mostly. Nora helps them get clean if necessary, get a GED, reunite with family or get jobs—whatever they need, really."

Collier nodded in acknowledgement but didn't look away from Corey. "Who did you talk to?"

"Jeremy Landis. He lives there and manages the place, I think."

His eye twitched at the name. "You know him?"

"We've only just met. Do you?"

"No, but I have a message from him. Said he would like to speak with me. That's it." Collier stared at her for a long time. "And?"

Corey drew in a long breath. "And this isn't just my story to tell. Thayer will have information you'll need." Her eyes flicked to Kelly. "And Reverend Warren, too."

The muscles in Collier's jaw bunched as he clenched his teeth. "Goddamn it, Curtis, this is about the body, isn't it?"

"I don't know. Maybe—probably—yes."

"What the hell is going on?" he growled.

Corey shook her head helplessly. "Honestly, I'm not sure. Thayer wanted to…I was just trying to—"

"If Doc had been up front with me the other day and told me what she knew then would any of this have happened?"

Corey bristled. "If you had returned this kid's phone call, would that have prevented it? This isn't Thayer's fault. She maintained professional responsibility and integrity and got him to reach out to you. If this turns out to be connected, don't you dare even hint to her that you think she's responsible for what happened."

Collier snorted a breath and looked at Kelly. "Do I need to worry about this kid taking off?"

"No. I know him. Jeremy is a good guy and a good friend to Nora. He'll want to help."

"Fine. Let's move on for now." He gestured for Corey to continue. "Where did Wiley go when you left?"

She pointed down the path. "This way. Jeremy told her it was a shortcut to the street. I went back to Rachel's car to move it up the block and called Thayer."

They walked in silence for several minutes, flashlights darting up and down the dark path and into the sparse trees and shrubbery that lined the path.

"Sarge, over here." Kelly stopped, training his light off the path several yards. There were multiple footprints leading from the path to a trampled area of snow where the light also glinted off a couple of empty liquor bottles.

Collier shone his own light over the area where they could all clearly see evidence that people had been there recently—cigarette butts and urine colored snow. "Call for another unit. Get them to cordon off this area and get some techs out here to photograph and bag everything. No one else walks this path tonight until it's been processed. Wait here until they arrive and then meet us back at the reverend's house. And call your sister and tell her to let the residents of that house know that a crime has been committed and not to interfere or go anywhere."

He motioned Corey back down the path the way they came. "Show me what you saw from your car."

Collier listened intently as Corey walked him through what she saw and what she did when she saw the danger to Rachel. She took the opportunity as they made their way back to Nora's house to move Rachel's car off the sidewalk and park it properly.

Collier's unmarked patrol car sat out front with the grill lights still on, splashing red and blue lights across the nearly empty street. He turned them off. The opposite side of the street was the old city cemetery and on the street were churches, all locked for the night, and a smattering of closed businesses. A few cars driving by slowed in curiosity before moving on and the weather kept any pedestrians out of the way.

"You did all right, Curtis," he said when Corey finally finished up her retelling of the attack on Rachel. "Scared them off and kept things from being a lot worse."

"Maybe." Corey shuddered in the cold, her earlier adrenaline, kept alive by anger, now leaching out of her and leaving her chilled and drained. "Can we take this inside?"

"Yeah." He held open the gate and gestured her ahead of him.

Rachel was back on the sofa, a blanket around her shoulders and holding an icepack to the side of her face. She had steri-strips under her eye, now swollen shut, to close the wound. The blood had been cleaned up and Thayer sat next to her with a cup of coffee talking with Nora.

"Hey, Rach, you okay?" Corey asked as she shed her coat and gratefully accepted a steaming cup of coffee from Nora. "Thank you."

"Better." Rachel managed without moving her mouth too much and reopening her split lip or aggravating her sore jaw.

"Feel up to answering some questions?" Collier asked.

Rachel simply nodded in response and eased herself back against the sofa.

"I've held off giving her anything for pain until after you took your statement," Thayer said. "So, the quicker we take care of this the better I can take care of her."

"Got it. Thanks, Doc." Collier pulled out his notebook and shed his coat, hanging it over the back of a chair.

"Curtis gave me a good accounting of what she saw, but she was pretty far away, and in the car, so I need to know what you saw and heard from the beginning."

"Not much."

"When did you first become aware you were being followed?"

"When I got hit from behind," she ground out angrily.

"You didn't see them before then? On the path or by the church?"

"If I had, I sure as fuck wouldn't have let myself get jumped like that. It was cold. I had my hood up and—" Her gaze darted quickly to Nora who was watching her with concern. "—I was distracted."

Collier saw her look and followed her gaze, but clearly understood what was going on. "Okay. Tell me about them. Could you identify them?"

"No. I don't know. Maybe. There were three of them. Well, four, I guess, but only three of them were taking shots at me. They reeked of booze. They were big, white, no facial hair, dressed all in black, I think. Sweatshirts with the hoods pulled up and dark pants or jeans. I didn't get a good look at faces. It all happened so fast."

"Plain black on the clothes? No logos or anything?"

She frowned. "Um, I don't know, maybe. If there was it was dark, too, but now that you ask there might have been something—I didn't really see."

Kelly slipped back in on a blast of cold air and headed straight for the coffee giving Collier a nod of acknowledgement. "Tell me more about the men?"

"Men? I don't know about that."

"What do you mean, Rach?" Corey asked. "The little one was a woman, I think for sure, but the others were definitely men."

"I mean, they were clumsy and soft—awkward moving and hesitant. They were big, and if they had known what they were doing I'd be in the hospital or the morgue." She glanced at Corey and shrugged. "They packed a punch from size alone but I don't think they've had any kind of training or even experience fighting. When I fought back they didn't know what to do and the one dickhead I racked squealed like a stuck pig."

Collier considered this. "You think kids?"

"I think so, yeah."

"Did they say anything?" Collier went on.

Rachel grunted. "Just a string of homophobic slurs—faggot, cocksucker, queer—and a bunch of other stupid nonsense shit."

"What about dyke?" Collier asked.

"What?" Corey glared at him and both Thayer and Nora visibly stiffened at the question.

He held up his hand. "Take it easy. I mean, they were rattling off their best hate speech but they didn't call you a dyke? Why not?"

Nora spoke into the long silence. "They thought she was a man. They thought you were Jeremy. You came from the house. You have a similar build, and even the same coat. Oh, god, it was dark and with your hood up..." She trailed off, eyes bright with tears as she looked at Rachel. Her voice, usually so carefully modulated, was now rough with emotion. "I am so sorry, Rachel."

"It's not your fault, Nora," Rachel said.

Collier turned his laser stare on Nora Warren. "Why would they want to hurt Jeremy?"

"Why?" Nora met his gaze with a piercing one of her own. "Because they're sadistic, hate-filled little bastards growing up in a gun and rape culture, whose behavior is not just protected, but lauded by the religious right. Cis-het, white males are emboldened in today's political climate to feel victimized by everyone not like them. They are taught to believe they are entitled to whatever they want. And they take it, regardless of who it oppresses or hurts and whose behavior is excused by bullshit beliefs like white nationalism, the 'boys will be boys' attitude, and the cult of the religious right."

"Damn, Nora," Kelly muttered. His surprised expression at his sister's outburst suggested she wasn't known for swearing and losing her temper.

"Don't act so shocked, little brother. Wasn't it just you talking about the growing packs of young men abusing drugs and terrorizing the city this summer, throwing rocks through storefronts and…" She trailed off, her gaze flicking back to Rachel when she made the connection to the vandalism.

It hadn't occurred to Corey until now, but Rachel did seem an unintentional magnet for idiot punks. Her eyes darted around the small room to see Thayer nodding in agreement and Rachel gazing at Nora adoringly.

Corey was beginning to see the similarities between Nora Warren and Thayer. More often than not she was even tempered, patient, thoughtful and calm under pressure. All were traits that would certainly serve her well in her line of work where, much like Thayer treated people's physical health, she tended to their spiritual well-being.

Now though, in the face of threats to people she cared about, she was impassioned and intense in defense of her flock.

Collier studied Nora Warren for a long moment before his eyes flicked to Corey.

"Don't look at me. We just met," Corey said. "But we're going to get along just fine."

"You know who they are?" Collier returned his attention to Nora.

"No. But I've suspected for a while now something was going on with Jeremy. He's not been himself. I don't know if it involves any of the other boys. My guess, knowing him, is he's protecting them, and I suppose me, by not talking openly about it or seeking help."

"We'll need to speak with him," Collier stated.

"Not without me," she said.

Kelly straightened off the counter. "He's an adult, Nora. I know he's your friend but you can't interfere in a possible homicide."

"Homicide?" Nora's mouth gaped. "What are you talking about? Who's dead?"

Rachel jerked forward in surprise, biting down on a hiss of pain. "The fuck?"

"Whoa. Rachel, don't move around like that." Thayer encouraged her to sit back. "You're done with Rachel for now, Jim?" she asked as she rummaged in her bag for a blister pack.

"For now, yeah. As soon as we get an I.D. on these guys, we'll see what we need to get them in for a line-up."

Thayer popped out two tabs and held them out. "Tylenol with codeine."

Rachel shook her head. "I want to know what the hell is going on."

"Please," Thayer said, then added, "I insist."

Rachel downed the tabs with a glass of water Corey handed her. "You'll run me home?"

"Of course." Thayer encouraged Rachel to lie down on her right side and pulled her boots off. "Just take it easy, now."

Corey grabbed a throw blanket off the back of the couch and covered her with it before perching protectively on the arm of the sofa by her head.

"You love me," Rachel teased her, fighting a smile to protect her split lip.

"Shut up." Corey smiled.

CHAPTER TWENTY-ONE

Corey shifted on the arm of the sofa to get more comfortable. Things were about to get serious—or more serious—now that the connection to the body was emerging.

"Nora, you mind if I make another pot of coffee?" Kelly asked and wandered into the kitchen area.

"You know where everything is." Nora gestured vaguely toward the pot as she pulled out a chair in the dining area and dropped wearily into it.

Collier pulled out the chair his coat was hanging over and settled his large frame into it, looking like he was prepared for this to take a while. Kelly remained leaning against the kitchen counter.

Collier wasted no time in getting down to business from the beginning. "Am I right, Doc, in assuming that Jeremy Landis was the patient you wrote the prescription for on Christmas Eve? The torn prescription we later found in the pocket of the unidentified deceased still thawing in the morgue?"

"That's correct," Thayer said unapologetically.

"When did you get in contact with Mr. Landis again?" he went on.

"Yesterday evening."

"Why?"

"I was concerned. He was sick and I knew at that point he wouldn't be able to have the prescription filled. Also, I thought I could help by encouraging him to reach out to you. I thought he would."

"He did," Corey said when it didn't appear Collier was going to admit to the message. She wanted Thayer to know Jeremy had done the right thing.

"I haven't spoken to him, yet," Collier admitted. "What was he sick with?"

Thayer hesitated and Corey knew she was uncomfortable discussing a patient's treatment.

"I don't see how it's relevant but the medicine I prescribed is commonly used to treat upper respiratory infections, among other things."

Corey smiled inwardly at her carefully worded answer, telling him what he wanted to know without directly violating Jeremy's right to privacy. Thayer made her decision to keep her patient's confidence and she would stand by it despite what had happened tonight. Corey supported her and was proud of her. She wasn't sure if Rachel had put all the pieces together yet and figured out Thayer's involvement in this mess, but she would talk to her about it when she was feeling better and make sure she wasn't angry with Thayer.

She took a moment to study Nora, whose expression wavered between curious and concerned. She still hadn't connected all the dots but remained calm and quiet, listening intently. The only hint of anxiety she displayed was the constant spinning of her coffee mug in slow circles on the table and her worried glances at Rachel.

Collier went on with his questioning of Thayer. "When you treated him at the hospital what did you and Jeremy Landis talk about?"

"His health."

"Anything else?"

"My bone structure," she said without a hint of humor, eliciting a quiet laugh from Nora. Even Kelly cracked a smile. Since they knew Jeremy they obviously got the joke.

Collier frowned like he couldn't quite tell if he was being made fun of. "Did he give you any indication he was being threatened?"

"None."

"Did he say anything to lead you to believe he was a threat to anyone else?"

"Absolutely not. If I had thought there was any chance, no matter how remote, that he was *in* danger or *a* danger to himself or anyone else, I would've called the police at the time or identified him to you when you asked."

After a long moment Collier nodded. "Did he mention where he was going after the hospital?"

"He said he was going home for Christmas Eve dinner with his family."

"Not to the pharmacy?"

"He mentioned he thought the pharmacy would be..." She covered her mouth with her hand.

"What?" Collier pressed.

Thayer cleared her throat after a long moment. "Nothing, um, he said the pharmacy near the church would still be open."

Corey frowned at Thayer's hesitation, knowing she had just made the connection between what happened tonight and the punks that had been hassling her outside the pharmacy before Christmas. She had hoped Thayer would say something, but now it seemed like she was going to keep it to herself. One more thing for her to be burdened by. In her state of mind of late, Corey would not be surprised if Thayer believed, by running into those boys the other night, she could have done something to prevent all this. "I think we saw them the other night," Corey stated.

"What?" Collier said, and all eyes turned to her except Thayer's whose head hung, her mouth closed tightly in a grim line.

"It doesn't really add much to the story at this point, but I think we saw these jerk-offs when we were running errands before Christmas. I guess it was the twenty-third. They were hanging around the pharmacy."

"Doing what?" Collier asked as he scribbled more notes.

Corey shrugged, her eyes flicking to Thayer. "Just being assholes and giving people a hard time. Cat-calling and whatever."

Collier looked up then, his gaze moving between Corey and Thayer, no doubt filling in the blanks of what was being left unsaid. "All right. We'll come back to that if we need to. Doc, when you spoke with Jeremy yesterday what did you say to him?"

Thayer took a deep breath. "That I knew he would not be able to fill his prescription so I brought him the medicine he needed. I told him I suspected something had happened to him after he left the hospital and so did the police. He needed to speak with you immediately. I gave him your card and told him that if he did not get in touch with you, that I would. I told him you were a friend and he could trust you."

"And what was his response to that?"

She shrugged slightly. "He was agitated but he understood, and he assured me he was going to call you in the morning."

"Did he tell you what happened?"

"I think he wanted to, but I told him it was best if he didn't tell me anything and just spoke with you and Kelly about it."

"You didn't mention the body to him?"

"No. That wasn't for me to disclose."

Collier eyed her with what Corey interpreted as admiration. "Do you think he was aware whatever interaction he had with this man may have resulted in his death?"

"With respect, Jim, we don't yet know there was any interaction between them," she argued. "However, his level of anxiety did not indicate he was aware someone had died."

"Okay," Collier finally said. "Thanks, Doc."

"I have a question for you," Thayer said. "When did Jeremy call you?"

Collier's jaw clenched and unclenched and Corey understood what it would cost him to admit he may have dropped the ball on his end. "The message came in this morning. I didn't listen to it until late this afternoon," he said finally.

"Reverend Warren." Collier turned to her. "I have a few questions for you, as well."

"Of course," she straightened in her chair.

"What is your relationship with Jeremy Landis?"

"We're friends and coworkers."

"Good friends?" he asked.

Corey guessed he was trying to gauge whether or not she would protect him and under what circumstances.

"Yes, good friends." Nora didn't seem concerned at the reason behind the question.

"Did you know he went to the ED Christmas Eve?"

"Yes, I encouraged him to go. He hadn't been feeling well for several days, and with all the boys in the house it was important he take care of himself. There were already a couple others showing signs of illness and I wasn't going to take a chance it could be something more serious."

"Was he late coming home?"

"Late? He was going to emergency. He could have been gone for days—" Her eyes flicked to Thayer. "Sorry. I wasn't expecting him at any particular time."

Thayer shrugged it off.

"He wanted to be back in time for Christmas Eve dinner and he was."

"And when he came back did you notice anything out of the ordinary?"

She considered for a moment. "He was out of breath and coughing a lot. I asked him about it and he said he had run from the bus stop trying to get to the pharmacy before it closed and then run back here to make it in time for dinner."

"You believed him?"

"I had no reason not to. I still don't."

"Okay." Collier tipped his head in acknowledgment. "Tell me about him. How do you know him?"

"How does that matter?"

Collier sucked in a long breath and sat back. "Look, we need to get something straight here."

Corey couldn't help a snort of amusement and earned herself glares in varying degrees of severity from everyone but Rachel, whose face she couldn't see but who was shaking with silent laughter.

"Watch it," Collier barked and jabbed a finger toward them. "At this time you two are not the ones on my radar for interfering in an active homicide investigation, but I'll gladly reconsider."

Corey fought against another laugh when Rachel muttered something about being in the "upside down." Thayer sighed audibly, crossing her arms and looking like it was painful to keep from rolling her eyes at the implied threat.

Collier's face reddened with anger and he glowered around the room. "That's right. You all think this is some damn joke? That there is no way your boy could be involved in anything criminal, but there's a body in the morgue, and CCTV video that shows him in an altercation with the deceased that says different." He gestured toward Rachel. "And a likely-related assault on one of your own."

"What video?" Thayer asked and looked at Corey. "Did you know?"

Corey shrugged helplessly.

"Why would she know? You think I just go around sharing details of ongoing investigations? This—" Collier gestured, dramatically around the room, "—this little tea party is what gets cases thrown out of court and officers put on suspension for mishandling investigations. I was giving you all the friends and family courtesy but we're done with all that now. It's long past time we go have a little chat with Mr. Landis down at the station." He pushed himself from the chair and nodded to Kelly.

Nora shot out of her chair. "Wait. Wait. You can't. Kelly, don't, please."

Kelly reached for Nora's hand. "Nora, it will be okay. We will be respectful and we won't—"

"Warren, explain," Collier ordered.

He sighed. "Sarge, these kids, they've been through a lot."

"They know you're a cop, right?"

"Yes. But they never see me in uniform. It can be…"

"Triggering," Nora finished for him. "Sergeant Collier, please believe I'm not trying to interfere with your investigation, but these kids have been through more trauma than anyone should face in their lifetime. Betrayal, abandonment and abuse in all forms and from virtually everyone they should've been able to trust—family, friends, teachers, the church and yes, the police. That house is a safe space for them and if you storm in there…" Her voice wavered with emotion.

Collier held out a calming hand. "First of all, no one is storming anything. We're professional and I'm sure you trust your brother—"

"It won't matter," Nora said desperately. "The only reason they're probably not halfway out the door right now with the police presence around is because Jeremy is talking them down."

Nora let out a slow, deliberate breath into the silence, her right hand going to her chest over her heart and her left covering her eyes. She whispered a few words not intended for the ears of anyone in the room. "I'm sorry," she sighed and sat back down. "I realize that isn't your problem. You're just doing your job and I appreciate that, I do."

Corey bit down hard on the inside of her cheek to keep from unleashing on Collier and she could see, by the tense set of Thayer's shoulders, she was keeping what she had to say clamped down, as well. Though she couldn't see her face, Corey could imagine Rachel's glare in his direction as he stood, jaw set, staring into the middle distance while he considered his next move.

Apparently having come to a decision, he pulled his phone and turned away to make a call. "This is Sergeant Jim Collier of the Jackson City Police returning your call. Am I speaking with Jeremy Landis?" He nodded once at the reply. "Mr. Landis, in a matter of minutes Officer Warren and Reverend Warren will be at your door to escort you back to Reverend Warren's home to meet with me and answer some questions regarding your whereabouts on Christmas Eve. In addition, I am seeking any information about an assault that took place an hour ago on the street in front of the Reverend's residence. Do you agree to cooperate with us?" He nodded again and turned back around, pocketing his phone.

Corey released the breath she had been holding and her eyes flicked to Thayer who offered her a relieved smile. Nora's eyes shone with emotion as she looked at Collier. "Thank you, Sergeant."

Collier grunted. "He'll likely be more forthcoming if he's comfortable."

Corey caught his gaze and arched a brow at his flimsy attempt to brush off his obvious act of compassion.

"Well, get going Warrens," he barked.

Thayer picked up her medical bag. "I'd like to go to too, if I may. I'd like to check out the boys you said weren't feeling well."

"You don't have to do that, Thayer," Nora said. "There's a walk-in clinic we can take them to."

She was already putting on her coat. "I'm here, I have everything I need, and I'd like to help."

Nora smiled gratefully. "Thank you. It will be good for them to have someone there right now."

Thayer reached for Corey's hand as she moved to stand in front of her. She kissed the back of her hand and held Corey's gaze intensely.

"You, too," Corey said to Thayer's unspoken words.

"Please, will the two of you refrain from doing anything ill-conceived for the next little while?" Thayer said, looking between Corey and Rachel.

Rachel laughed. "You know I would do anything for you but you may be asking the impossible."

"Do this then. Close your eyes and get some rest."

"Eye," Corey deadpanned.

"Yeah, thanks, idiot," Rachel shot back.

"Doc?" Collier gestured toward the door, impatiently.

"Sorry, yes, I'm going."

Corey crouched down in front of Rachel as soon as the three of them were out the door. "Hey, you okay?"

"Yeah." Rachel winced a little when she shifted to a more comfortable position. "Pills are helping."

"That's good. Need anything else?"

"I feel like a fucking dickhead getting my ass kicked like that right in front of her house. Jesus, what a way to make an impression."

"Simmer down, Xena, I'm pretty sure you don't have anything to be embarrassed about. There were three goons twice your size taking cheap shots at you from behind and you still got your licks in. And, for what it's worth, this is how Thayer and I got our start—me bleeding all over her house in a drug-induced stupor on our first failed date."

"So, you're saying there's hope for me?"

"I'm saying, once all the swelling goes down she'd be a fool not to suck your face off."

"Ow, it hurts when I laugh. Looks like you'll be working out with Emma for a while."

Corey cringed. "Don't ever say that again."

Rachel's smile faltered and her breath shuddered. "That really sucked."

Corey's throat tightened with emotion. "I know. For me, too. If something ever happened to you…"

"Something did happen to me."

"Something irreversible, I mean."

"You'd go crazy with grief, shave your head, and hoard cats?"

"Nah. I may miss a meal with stress-induced reflux, but I'd bounce."

Rachel fought another painful laugh. "Good thing it didn't come to that."

"Good thing."

"You want more coffee, Curtis?" Collier asked from the kitchen.

"Yeah." She stood and gave Rachel's shoulder a gentle squeeze. "Close your eye."

"Shut up," Rachel sighed, but did as she was told.

"Thanks." Corey retrieved her cup and let Collier refill it from the fresh pot of coffee he'd brewed. She eyed him over her cup. "So, here we are again."

He sipped his own coffee. "At least the coffee's good. We could be here for a while."

"You're not kicking us out?"

He grunted. "What's that saying about closing the barn door after the horse has bolted? Seems like it applies." He nodded toward the sofa. "Anyway, doesn't look like Wiley should be moving around too much, right now. She okay?"

"She's tough, and not that it makes this better or anything, but Rachel's been in some worse scrapes. She may be young, but that girl has lived."

"Not at all surprised. She's a survivor."

Corey glanced back to see Rachel already asleep. "I hope you know this is not what I wanted to have happen. Thayer was just trying to do the right thing for her job and to help this kid *and* you. And well, you were right about her struggling with feeling—"

"I'm sorry, what was that?" He arched a brow at her and slurped his coffee noisily.

Corey groaned and rolled her eyes. "You were right."

He smiled triumphantly. "Carry on with what you were saying, Curtis."

She shook her head and fought a smile. "I'm sorry for... for whatever this is. I was just trying to be supportive, and incidentally I tried to tell you yesterday morning. And now, Rachel..."

"She was hoping to have a religious experience?"

"Something like that." Corey barked a laugh, then sobered. "I honestly don't know how it went sideways so fast."

"I assume you'll be cool if I take the lead from here?"

"Shit, yes." She grinned, crookedly. "As long as you let me do the autopsy."

"You can still have that part. Any idea when?"

"Tomorrow."

CHAPTER TWENTY-TWO

Jeremy's gaze darted nervously around the living room from Collier to Corey and eventually stopping on Rachel asleep on the sofa. "Is she going to be okay?"

Corey moved back over to the sofa and perched on the arm by Rachel's head. "She'll be all right, Jeremy. Don't worry about that."

"Mr. Landis." Collier extended his hand. "I'm Sergeant Jim Collier. We just spoke."

Jeremy's eyes widened at the respectful greeting and shook his hand. "Hello."

"Why don't you have a seat." Collier gestured to one of the two chairs at the small table.

"Thank you." Jeremy sat dutifully and cleared his throat, his voice still raspy from illness.

"I'm going to make you some tea, Jer." Nora filled and electric kettle and turned it on, leaning against the counter with Kelly.

"Um, thanks." He straightened in his chair when Collier took the chair across from him and pulled out his notebook.

"I understand you haven't been feeling well," Collier began.

"It's not serious," he replied earnestly.

"Serious enough to send you to the Emergency Department on Christmas Eve?"

"Yeah, um, yes, Nora wanted me to get checked out."

"Why don't we start there. What time did you arrive at the hospital?"

"Uh, I took the three-seventeen bus. I wanted to be home in time for dinner."

"Okay. What time were you seen?"

"I don't know exactly. I think I got called to a room about an hour later for vitals. Then I waited to go to X-ray. I think it was around five thirty when I finally saw Thayer, er, Dr. Reynolds."

"Okay. We can verify all that with the hospital." Collier jotted notes in his book.

Jeremy shifted uncomfortably. "You think I'm lying?"

"No, I don't. But in cases such as these we need to get as accurate a timeline as possible for all the persons involved."

"Persons involved in what?" Jeremy's gaze darted around the room again, finding Nora, who could only offer him a supportive smile.

"We'll get to that. How long were you with Dr. Reynolds?"

"Less than half an hour," Jeremy said with confidence. "She wrote me a prescription and I caught the six-twelve bus back to Church Street."

"And you went straight back to AllWays House?"

Jeremy squirmed visibly. "Um, no, I went to the Towne Plaza to the drugstore. I thought the pharmacy would still be open but it closed at six."

Collier set his book aside, eyeing Jeremy seriously. "Tell me what happened at the pharmacy."

"Here you go, honey." Nora set a steaming mug of tea in front of him and rubbed a hand across his back. "It's okay. Whatever happened, you're not alone."

Jeremy nodded and cupped his hands around the mug, staring into it. "There are these guys that hang out around the bowling alley. They're there a lot, not doing anything but being racist, bigoted, asshole punks—harassing girls, picking fights with other boys, drinking and smoking."

"How many of them are there?"

"Four usually, sometimes more, but four regulars. And sometimes there's this girl with them—a girlfriend of one of them, I think. She's actually the worst—getting them all wound up and cheering them on when they go after someone."

"You know their names?" Collier asked.

"One of them might be Roy or Ray and one of them they call Bull, whatever that means." He shook his head. "They're from JC High."

"They're high schoolers?" Collier's gaze darted to Kelly.

"That will help narrow the search. Thank you." He jotted down his own notes.

"Well, they used to be, at least," Jeremy said. "They're always wearing the stupid Black Jacket sweatshirts. Probably voted most likely to succeed. It's always those losers—the spoiled rich kids that dropped out of college after the first year because they couldn't cut not being the most popular anymore."

"You've run into them before?" Collier asked.

"All the time." Jeremy laughed humorlessly. "They think I'm pretty."

"I'll look into reports of trespassing, loitering or public disturbance for the area," Kelly offered.

"Oh, hey," Corey interrupted. "Sorry, but Rachel mentioned the other day that the owners of the bowling alley had filed some complaints."

"I'll check it out." Kelly nodded his thanks.

"Oh, Jeremy, why didn't you come to me?" Nora asked.

"What would you have done, Nora?" Jeremy asked, helplessly. "It's nothing that any of us haven't faced before. Aren't I supposed to be the leader? Setting the good example on how to not to let the dicks get you down?"

"Not by putting yourself in danger," Nora argued.

"What danger?" Jeremy asked.

Nora shook her head, her gaze going to Rachel, her brow furrowing with concern.

"What happened Christmas Eve?" Collier redirected the conversation back to the facts.

Jeremy shrugged. "The usual. I was in a hurry so I wasn't being very cautious. I know to keep my eye out for them and try and keep a low profile or wait until they're distracted by something else. Honestly, it doesn't take that much—they're really dumb. Like orcs." He sucked in a long breath and paused to drink his tea. "Anyway, I rushed down to the pharmacy but it was closed. I headed around to the back of the plaza, intending to cut up the hill that leads into the cemetery instead of going all the way around to the road. They followed me around to the back and started giving me a hard time."

"A hard time how?" Collier asked.

"Taunting, name calling, obscene gestures and just general drunken fuckery."

"Did they assault you?" Collier prodded.

"Uh, no, not really. Fucking cowards."

"You'd rather they had?" Nora said angrily. "Look what they did to Rachel. They likely thought she was you."

"Easy, Nora," Kelly muttered, laying a hand on her arm.

Jeremy's eyes welled at Nora's words. "I'm sorry. I don't know. They've never come after me like that before. They were only ever all talk and scare tactics."

"I'm sorry," Nora said. "This isn't your fault and I'm grateful you weren't hurt."

"What do you mean by scare tactics?" Collier went on.

"Getting up in my face, faking like they were going to hit me, snatching the prescription out of my hand and ripping it up, chasing me if I ran—just schoolyard bully bullshit."

"Did they chase you that night?" Collier asked.

"One of them did. That's how I know they call him Bull. The others were cheering him on. The girl was there, too. I think he's the boyfriend."

"What happened?"

"I scrambled up the hill behind the plaza to the cemetery like I planned. It's steep and really slippery and he was really drunk. I don't think he could make the climb. I never saw what happened to him."

"What about the others?"

"No idea. I took off through the cemetery and back to the house. Took me like five minutes."

Collier finished writing in his notebook, closed it and slipped it back into his breast pocket. "Okay. Thank you, Mr. Landis. You've been very helpful."

"Wait." Jeremy's eyes flicked from him to Kelly to Nora. "That's it?"

"That's it." Collier nodded and stood.

"But why are you here?" Jeremy stood with him. "What's the crime? Was I suspected of something? Did those kids say *I* did something wrong? Did *they*?"

Corey eyed Collier, whose expression was relaxed, bordering on pleasant. Kelly was intensely stone faced and Nora looked confused at the change in tone. Corey knew what was happening. He wanted to gauge Jeremy's reaction to the news, and Collier proved her correct the next moment.

"We found a frozen body beneath a dumpster behind the plaza the day after Christmas. He had a piece of a prescription in his pocket that Dr. Reynolds has confirmed she wrote to you."

CHAPTER TWENTY-THREE

"What?" Jeremy paled, his voice barely a whisper, and dropped back into the chair. "How?"

"That still remains to be seen. His body was frozen but should be ready for autopsy tomorrow," Collier said.

Jeremy looked up to him, worriedly. "You think I had something to do with his death?"

"Did you?"

"No! No, I didn't. I ran. I never touched him."

"Okay, then. We'll know more after the autopsy."

Corey couldn't stand the silence that fell over the room. "Here's what's bugging me."

"Oh, here we go." Collier crossed his arms.

"If these clowns have been harassing Jeremy on the regular for however long but have never touched him, why did they decide to beat the piss out of him tonight?" She gestured to Rachel. "And why, by the way, has no one reported this guy Bull missing? Like, his buddies or his girlfriend. They would have known that he never returned to whatever rock they crawled out from under?"

"Unless they knew what happened to him," Kelly said.

"What?" Nora blurted aghast. "You're suggesting they knew he fell and was possibly injured and did nothing to help him?"

"Could have been what escalated them to violence," Kelly added. "The death of their friend."

Corey shook her head in disbelief. "Freezing to death wouldn't have happened instantly. It could have taken hours. They would have had more than enough time to get help for him. Can you get them on charges of, I don't know, failure to render aid or something?"

Kelly shook his head. "There's no 'duty to rescue' law in New York State. It's unequivocally shitty but not against the law not to help someone in distress unless you are a parent, spouse or employer. It's possible they couldn't find him if they'd all been drinking. It was dark, he was in black and his body was obscured by the dumpster."

"They blame Jeremy for whatever they think happened to their friend," Nora said. "That's why they attacked him—or rather, Rachel."

Corey eyed Collier. "Well?"

"I don't necessarily disagree with any of that, but none of it is provable or a prosecutable offense," he said.

"Since when isn't beating someone up against the damn law?" Corey asked angrily. "We're talking about a hate crime."

"Can you identify them? Can Rachel?"

Corey's lips pressed into a hard line. "No."

"I can," Jeremy said.

"Well, unfortunately or fortunately depending, they haven't done anything to you," Collier reminded him.

Jeremy pursed his lips. "What if they did?"

"What do you mean?" Collier asked.

"What if they were caught in an actual crime? Like trying to hurt someone?"

"What are you suggesting?"

"Can't we, you know, set up a sting or something?" Jeremy asked, eyes bright with excitement. "I mean they can't just get away with this. Now that they have a taste for it, especially if they're not even going to get in trouble, aren't they likely to do it again?"

"Probably." Collier nodded. "Eventually."

"Then why not give them an opportunity and catch them?"

"You've seen too many movies, kid."

"I could do it without you." Jeremy eyed him hard.

"Jeremy don't be absurd," Nora said. "You're not setting yourself up to be attacked."

"How is this any different than what we face every day? Just this time the police will be hanging around and catch them in the act."

"Jeremy, no," Nora said.

"I'm not a child, Nora."

Nora crossed her arms and shook her head. "Kelly, please, will you tell him?"

"I don't know, Nora, maybe it's not a bad idea. They went after him once already. Think about how pissed they're gonna be when they find out it wasn't him?" He looked at Collier. "Sarge?"

Collier considered. "What do you bet those idiots never wash their sweatshirts either. Bet Wiley's DNA is all over them."

"You can't be serious," Nora snapped. "Don't you have rules against putting a civilian in harm's way?"

"I choose this, Nora," Jeremy insisted. "I want to help."

"Just settle down, kid. I'll check with the ADA and find out what we need to make a case that will hold up, given everything we know now." Collier held out a staying hand. "We're calling it a night. Warren, please escort Mr. Landis back to his house."

Jeremy stood up. "But—"

"Jeremy, please," Nora said softly. "We all appreciate your willingness to help but the best way for you to do that now is to go back to the house and speak with the guys, all right? Let's let the police do their job."

Jeremy looked, for a moment, like he was going to argue more but relented. "Yeah, okay." He crossed the room and Nora met him halfway pulling him into her arms. "I'm really sorry about your friend, Nora."

She ran her hands up and down his back comfortingly. "No one blames you, Jeremy." She pulled away to look at him. "You know that, right?"

He nodded but still looked on the verge of tears.

"Let Kelly take you home and get some rest, okay?" She gave him a gentle shove toward the door where Kelly was waiting. "We'll talk tomorrow."

"Will you make sure Thayer gets back here safely?" Corey asked Kelly.

"Absolutely."

"Now what?" Corey asked as Collier put his coat back on.

"Now I write up a report and meet you tomorrow. What time?"

"Let's say ten." Corey looked at Rachel. "I want to make sure Rach is okay tomorrow."

"I'll be there." Collier was out the door.

Corey looked Rachel over. She hadn't moved and was heavily asleep with the help of pain medication.

"You can leave her here," Nora said quietly.

"I'm not sure what to do. Let's wait for Thayer."

Thayer knocked quietly a few minutes later and slipped in, taking off her coat and kicking out of her boots. "Hey." She went immediately to Corey and wrapped her arms around her waist.

Corey held her tightly and kissed her temple. "You all right?"

"Yes." Thayer nodded against her chest. "Just exhausted."

"Thank you so much for doing that, Thayer," Nora said. "Are the guys all right?"

Thayer pulled away from Corey. "They were worried about Jeremy and pretty anxious about the police presence, but I did the best I could to assure them everything was all right."

"I should go over." Nora made a move toward her coat.

"I don't want to tell you what to do, but I don't think you need to, really," Thayer said. "They were pretty wound up when Jeremy came back with Kelly and wanted to know all about his interrogation. They'll probably be up for a while but they seemed more excited than anything."

"Okay." Nora moved back over to the table and dropped into a chair. "I'll trust your judgment."

"What about Rachel?" Corey asked Thayer. "Nora said she could stay, but I don't want to make that decision for her."

"Let me take a look." Thayer perched on the edge of the sofa next to her and touched the back of her hand to her forehead and took her pulse. She stirred only when Thayer raised her shirt and palpated around the ugly bruise on her back.

"Ow," she slurred and cracked an eye.

"Rachel, how do you feel?" Thayer asked and pulled her shirt down, covering her again with the blanket.

"Wrecked," she mumbled, already drifting back to sleep.

"Corey and I have to go. Nora has offered for you to stay here tonight or we can bring you home with us."

"What time is it?" Rachel whispered.

Thayer checked her watch. "Almost ten."

"Fuck." She sighed, her good eye opening again. "My turn to close."

"I'll call Lainey." Corey pulled out her phone.

"I don't think you should be alone tonight and I don't think you should move around if you don't have to," Thayer advised.

"Mm, 'kay," she murmured. "Stay."

Thayer brushed hair off her face and turned to Nora. "Can I see your phone?"

"Sure." Nora looked around, finally finding it on the kitchen counter and handing it over.

"I'm giving you my number, Corey's number, and Jim Collier's number in case you need anything." Her eyes flicked to Rachel and her lip twitched into the beginnings of a smile. "And Rachel's number while I'm at it." She handed the phone back and dug in her satchel, handing over the blister pack of meds. "Two more in four hours if she wakes up and is in pain."

"Yes, thank you." Nora placed the medication on the coffee table.

"I'll have Thayer drop me off before her shift at eight. Will you be up that early?" Corey asked.

"If I even sleep at all after this," Nora said.

"Are you a hugger?" Thayer asked, with an expectant smile.

"We take a class on it in seminary. Bring it in."

"Really?" Corey said. "That's so weird."

"She's joking, Corey." Thayer embraced her with the enthusiasm of old friends. "I'm very sorry for all this, Nora, but I'm very pleased to have met you."

Nora smiled. "I sure am glad to have you two on my side right now."

"Take care of our girl." Corey gave her a wave.

Nora canted her head, with a smile, but didn't comment on Corey's inclusion of her in Rachel's life.

CHAPTER TWENTY-FOUR

Rachel opened the door to Corey's soft knock early the next morning. "You look like shit, dude," Corey said. Rachel's face was discolored from jaw to eye.

"Thanks." She stepped back from the door with a slight limp, favoring her left side.

"Where's Nora?" Corey looked around. The throw blanket had been folded neatly and the cushions straightened on the sofa. "Thought she'd be nursing you back to health."

"Haven't seen her. Can you try not to be an idiot for ten minutes and help me find my boots?"

"You wanna just bail? Thought I could at least get a cup of coffee for my trouble."

"What trouble? You can get a coffee at the shop." Rachel lowered herself back onto the sofa to wrestle on her boots.

"First of all, before you do that, I'm under strict instructions to make you use the bathroom. And be honest, I don't want to have to inspect your pee. If you're bleeding, I'm to take you to see Thayer at work."

"Fine." Rachel held out her hand. "Help me up."

Corey pulled her to her feet, slowly. "Second of all, I am to tell you that you are to take it easy today and if you give me any shit about it, I'm to remind you that you have a party to host in two days and if you want Thayer to help you with make-up to cover the evidence of your misfortune, heed her advice."

"Jesus," Rachel muttered as she limped back toward the bathroom. "She really said that?"

"She made me repeat it back to her. I'm going to make coffee. Even if we jet, the least we can do is have it ready for Nora. She's kinda gone above and beyond."

"Just doing what any friend would have," Nora said softly from behind her a moment later.

Corey whirled around, filters in one hand and grounds in the other. "Oh, hey." Nora was dressed in flowy, striped, jammy pants and a nonmatching, oversize shirt. Her hair was loose and in disarray around her shoulders. Even clearly sleep deprived and rumpled she really was lovely and seemed to glow with a natural, effortless warmth. "I hope this is okay," Corey blurted, shaking herself back to the moment.

"'Course." She smiled sleepily. "I'm sorry I wasn't up. It took me a really long time to unwind and I was worried about Rachel." Her eyes darted around as if just realizing she wasn't there.

Corey went back to making coffee. "She's just in the bathroom. Thayer gave me very explicit instructions to pass along to her."

"It's nice when your partner feels about your friends like you do. It doesn't always work out like that. I've known some relationships that didn't survive those types of conflicts."

Corey barked a laugh. "Most of my friends like Thayer better than they like me, so it works out well. And Rachel and I share the same brain most times, so it's not out of Thayer's way to care about her, too. Even so, Thayer's got the biggest heart of anyone I've ever known."

"I've noticed."

"Except for maybe you," Corey added. "A big heart, I mean."

Nora cocked her head. "So, I meet with your approval?"

"Are you looking for it?"

Nora's gaze flicked toward the hallway as Rachel made her way back to the living room. She didn't answer, but a small smile played at her lips before turning to a worried frown when Rachel stepped into the light and Nora could see the full extent of her injuries. "Oh, Rachel."

"Hot, huh?" She moved stiffly over to the chair across from Nora and sat gingerly. "No blood, Corey. As much as I like to look at Thayer, I don't need to see her again."

Corey plucked the pain tabs off the coffee table and tossed them in front of her. "She told me to make you take these, too." She placed a mug of coffee in front of Rachel and Nora pulled milk and sugar from the fridge.

"Christ, you'd think she was my girlfriend. Is she like this with you?"

"You mean thoughtful and caring? Yes. Take the pills."

Rachel tossed back the meds with a swallow of coffee. "So, what did I miss last night?"

"Collier arrested Thayer for obstruction of justice," Corey quipped.

"Oh, great, just when I was starting to like that prick."

Corey laughed. "I'm kidding, but I like how you thought that was a thing that could happen."

"Very funny. It's not like there isn't precedence."

Nora looked startled. "Thayer's been arrested?"

"No. Corey." Rachel jabbed a finger at her. "For being an idiot."

Nora grunted. "Were that a crime maybe we wouldn't be dealing with all this."

"What are we dealing with?" Rachel asked. "I feel kinda out of the loop."

Corey looked at her watch. "I'll tell you about it in the car. I'm posting the guy this morning and I want to get photos and do the external before Collier gets there. He's going to be on a tear, I'm sure."

"Yeah, sure." Rachel pushed herself to her feet.

"Actually, Rachel," Nora said. "If you'd like to stay for a little while, I can make us some breakfast and I can fill you in. I have time. I can drive you home later."

"Oh, um, thanks, Nora. You've done way more than enough."

"I don't think I've done nearly enough, but actually, I was kind of hoping you'd do something for me."

"What?"

"I know it's a huge ask and you're not feeling well, but I was hoping you would come up to the house with me. Jeremy was really worried about you and he's already been texting me this morning about how you're doing. I told him this wasn't his fault, but I know he feels responsible. I think it would help if he and the rest of the guys could see you're all right, or as all right as you can be given the circumstances."

"Oh, Nora, I don't know."

"I totally understand. Last night must have been terrible for you. Forgive me. I should never have asked. You must be exhausted and—"

"That's not it. I mean, yes, I'm tired, but I've passed a mirror and I'm looking pretty rough. I don't think those guys should see me like this."

Nora smiled sadly. "There's no act of violence or hate they're not already intimately familiar with, I'm afraid. What they could use more of in their lives are good queer role models, especially from right in their own community. Folks that have succeeded despite the adversities and obstacles they've faced and I can think of no one better than you. And I don't just mean after what happened last night. I mean you're an outstanding success, not *in spite* of who you are, but *because of* who you are. I was hoping, maybe, you'd share yourself with them—with me."

Rachel opened and closed her mouth a couple of times, looking shocked at Nora's description of her, but she didn't manage to form a word.

Nora waited expectantly for a beat before she winced. "I just assumed way too much didn't, I?" She covered her face with her hands and mumbled. "I'm so sorry. I don't know what's gotten into me."

"What?" Rachel frowned her gaze flicking to Corey.

Corey fought a laugh and mouthed the word "queer."

"Oh. Oh, no, you're cool, Nora. It was the 'outstanding success' part that threw me, not 'queer.' I identify like that sometimes. I mean, not sometimes I'm *queer*, but sometimes I use that word as opposed to others like *pan* or *omni*. I mean, honestly I don't keep up with the terminology and I don't care—I mean, of course, I care. Everyone should be able to identify in the ways that they're comfortable. I'm just not that particular."

Corey grimaced and slashed her hand in the air in a cut-off motion.

Rachel smiled apologetically. "Please, tell me the drugs have kicked in. Oh, my god, I'll show myself out."

Nora dropped her hands. "You're leaving?"

"No, I meant...It was just an expression."

Corey covered her face with her hand and shook her head. "Rachel?"

"Right, okay. Sorry, yeah."

Nora's brows rose. "Yeah, you'll stay for a while and come up to the house?"

"Sure, yeah, but I'm kinda dopey from the meds, so I don't know what crazy shit might come out of my mouth—as evidenced by my word salad thus far."

"As long as it's truth, that's all I ask," Nora replied.

Corey clapped her hands together. "Okay, great. Glad we got that settled. I'm taking your car. You can pick it up at the morgue whenever. I'll leave the keys in it. I'll come by to see you after work."

CHAPTER TWENTY-FIVE

Corey was surprised to see Cin sitting at the computer when she came into the morgue. "I wasn't expecting you today. What's up?"

She closed down her email. "I needed a break. I was losing perspective and needed to get away from my writing for a while. Got anything going on today?"

"As a matter of fact, I do. We're posting the frozen guy this morning. Collier will be by in a while, but I'm going to bust out the external. Wanna get him out for me? I gotta throw on scrubs."

Cin hopped up and moved into the autopsy suite. "Sounds wonderfully distracting."

"What do you see?" Corey asked when the body was on the table.

Cin walked around the body, looking it over from head to toe. "Deceased, but otherwise healthy looking, well-fed, white male in his late teens or early twenties. No external signs of trauma. No bruising, no evidence of surgical scars." She raised his eyelids and pried open his mouth. "No evidence of petechiae in the mucosal tissues, good oral hygiene. Clipped and clean fingernails, and no evidence of I.V. drug use."

"Not very exciting, but telling in what isn't there, right? He's likely not an addict or homeless, and there's no recent physical injury that would explain his current condition. Let's get some more photos." She passed the camera to Cin.

They were finishing up the external exam when the buzzer rang. "That'll be Collier," Corey said.

"Where we at, Curtis?" he said as he and Kelly came in, shaking off the cold.

"Ready to cut. Just waiting for the big boss man. You have anything new?"

"Yep." He sat in the chair to pull on booties over his boots. "With the Landis kid's partial names to go by we got a tentative I.D. Jonathan Bullard, Bull to his friends. Twenty years old, graduated JC High two years ago, second string football, voted class clown. Got his picture from the yearbook."

"His mother died ten years ago of breast cancer and his father travels frequently for business," Kelly went on. "Jonathan and his older sister live at the family home. We're attempting to contact the father."

"What about his buddies?" she asked.

"Can't know for sure until we get eyes on them, but we have some ideas based on who he's with in the yearbook photos. We're looking into the possibilities," Collier finished as Dr. Webster came in.

"We ready to go?" he asked. "I don't have a lot of time."

"External and photos are done," Corey said. "Cin's setting up the tray now."

Corey leaned over the freshly opened body and pulled her mask down over her nose. "Whoa, rank." She sniffed and shook her head.

Collier looked up from his notetaking. "What?"

She pulled her mask back on. "Tequila. Dude reeks of booze."

Cin was collecting vitreous from the eye and blood from the aorta, which was thick and sluggish. "Bladder is empty," she said after spending a moment unsuccessfully fishing around with the long needle.

Dr. Webster came over and eyed the organs in situ. Everything was intact and injury free and there was no blood where there shouldn't be. "Let's start with the heart and lungs. They look boggy."

Corey removed the heart and lungs en bloc and set them on the tray for Dr. Webster to dissect. He opened the main stem bronchi and pink, frothy fluid poured out. The lungs were similarly dark, heavy and fluid filled. "Extensive pulmonary edema," he said.

"Meaning?" Collier asked.

"Heart failure. Extreme exposure to cold increases blood pressure, forcing fluid out through the capillary walls and causes ventricular fibrillation from disruption to the electrical system and cardiac arrest."

"So, he froze to death," Collier stated.

"Unless in the last few days you have discovered evidence that we need to be looking for something else, that is near certain," Webster replied. He sliced through the heart and opened the atria and ventricles along the path of blood flow, examining the muscles and valves.

Corey, anticipating his next request, plugged in the Stryker and cut through the calvarium she had already exposed by slicing through the scalp from ear to ear across the crown of the head.

She used the skull splitter to crack the top of the skull off. There were no skull fractures and no blood in the brain. The tissue was intact and healthy, aside from being dead. She quickly and skillfully removed the brain from the skull by slicing the nerves, vessels and spinal column at the foramen magnum.

Dr. Webster sliced the brain like a loaf of bread, laying out the slices on the cutting board and shrugged. "Nothing to see here," he said.

"Cause of death, then?" Collier asked.

Webster snapped off his gloves and pulled a death certificate from the drawer. He tapped a blue pen on the counter for a moment. "Hypothermia due to extreme and prolonged cold exposure and acute alcohol intoxication. Probably." He spoke aloud as he filled in the form and checked a box with a flourish. "Accident."

"Sort of anticlimactic," Kelly mumbled.

"Make sure you get all the labs sent off today, Corey," Webster said as he pulled his gown off. "Send stomach contents as well and get the liver sections put through the processor on a rush from me."

"Will do." Corey took over the scalpel and began the rest of the evisceration while Cin scooped up the sections and started weighing the organs already out.

Collier went back to his notes and Kelly's phone rang. "It's Taggart," he announced.

"Take it," Collier commanded without looking up.

"Warren," he said and listened for a moment. "The sister? Yes, bring her down. We'll be ready." He hung up and eyed Corey. "Can we be ready?"

"For what?" Corey looked up from dissecting the kidneys. "Wait, that's who that was. I totally ran into Taggart on Christmas by Rachel's shop, like, literally he smacked into me—and stepped on my dog. I knew I recognized that idiot. I don't think he knew who I was."

"Well, now you can bitch him out. Monica Bullard is coming down with Officer Taggart to positively identify her brother's body," Kelly explained.

"When?" Corey dropped the right kidney into the pan for Cin to weigh.

"Twenty minutes."

"What?" Corey looked up, eyes wide over her mask and looked at the body, opened like a book with intestines literally hanging out of him, skull open and empty, body blood splattered. "What the fuck, you guys, come on."

Collier smiled grimly. "Work your magic, Curtis."

"Shit, okay. Cin, can you keep going with the dissection?"

"Sure, yep." She slid over in front of the bench.

Corey grabbed the calvarium and positioned it back onto his skull, folding the skin of his face and back of his head back into place and throwing in a quick stitch through the top of his head to keep it together.

She placed the chest plate back on and folded the flaps of skin and muscle back over his abdominal and chest cavities, grimacing at the look of his sunken body without any organs. She opened the body back up and grabbed a stack of towels from the cabinet, shaking them out before stuffing them into the body to fill it out. She closed him back up and stitched again in a couple of places to hold it all together.

She sponged off the blood from his face, chest and arms and wound a towel around his head as if he had just gotten out of the shower. She covered him with more towels and finally a clean sheet pulled up to his neck. "How's that?"

"Looks like he's sleeping," Kelly commented.

"Fine," Collier said.

Corey transferred the body back to the gurney and made a few final adjustments before wheeling the body out into the anteroom and locking the brakes. "I'm going to let you two take it from here. I need to finish up the dissection."

"Sure." Collier nodded as she ducked back into the autopsy suite and closed the door just as the buzzer sounded.

She leaned against the door, tipping her head back and listening to Collier's rumbling voice for a moment. She flinched at the anguished shriek of Jonathan Bullard's sister and moved her head off the door as her voice rose in rage-filled grief.

"He never fucking listens to me. He should have done what he was fucking told!" was the single intelligible sentence that filtered through before the morgue door opened and slammed so hard Corey winced at the vibration of it.

"Hey," Cin said quietly and placed a hand on her shoulder. "You okay?"

"Yeah. I hate this part."

"Come on. Let's finish up and I can take you out for a drink."

"I would love to but I can't. I gotta go check on Rach."

"Why does Rachel need checking on?" Cin stacked the brain slices and slid them onto the scale to be weighed.

Corey blew out a noisy breath. "It's a really long story."

Before Cin could speak again Collier came back in. "We're all set, Curtis."

"I take it it's him?"

"It is. She *claims* she hadn't seen him the night he died. He was out with his friends who, she *claims*, she doesn't know and can't identify, and it wasn't unusual for him to be gone for days."

"Why do you say it like that?"

"Brother and sister close in age living together, but don't know each other's friends? Not likely. I think we may be looking at the female member of this group. She seemed angrier than surprised to see him dead."

"So, what now?"

Collier shrugged. "We go back to the station, write this up and close out this case. The death was accidental. The father is on the way home and they'll be in touch with the funeral home, et cetera, et cetera. You know the drill better than I do."

"What about Rachel?"

"What about her?"

"I mean; is there something you can do about the rest of these assholes? They could have killed her."

Collier sucked on his teeth. "Let me finish this up and think about it some more. I've got a call in to the ADA and Warren is looking into any complaints coming from the plaza store owners. In the meantime, I'll make sure a car patrols the area and drives by the church and house several times overnight. I'm sorry, I wish there was more that I could do."

"I get it." Corey nodded and sighed heavily. "Thanks."

"Okay. I'll see you."

CHAPTER TWENTY-SIX

Corey locked up the morgue at five and stepped into the stairwell to see Thayer on her way down. "Perfect timing."

"Hi, sweetheart." Thayer stopped on the landing above and leaned against the railing. "How was your day?"

Corey climbed the stairs to meet her. "The usual. Death and decay with a side of next of kin's naked sorrow."

"That doesn't sound 'usual.' Are you all right?"

"Yeah, don't mind my melodrama." Corey slipped her arms around Thayer and pulled her close, sighing happily when Thayer returned the hug. "The sister of that kid came in to identify his body. Then overwhelming grief happened and that part is hard for me."

"That part is hard for everyone." Thayer smiled up at her and held her tighter.

"No, I know. That's the part I try to avoid so I can do what I do. Maybe you were right about what you said the other day. Maybe I do dehumanize to get through a case. I can't know them when they were alive, too. It's just too…much."

"No, I was *not* right, but I understand what you mean."
Thayer slid her hands behind Corey's head and tilted her face
for a gentle kiss. "You ready to get out of here?"

Corey lingered on Thayer's lips. "Just another minute." She
encouraged Thayer to let her in and deepened their kiss walking
them back toward the wall, one arm slipping around Thayer's
waist and the other hand tangling in the hair at her neck.

"Corey, not here," Thayer protested around the heat of her
kisses but didn't pull away.

Corey pressed into her for another moment before backing
off, licking her lips. "Sorry."

"Don't be sorry. Just take me home and then we can renew
our love and appreciation for life together."

"Hold that thought. We have to swing by and check on
Rachel first."

"Oh, I've never seen her place," Thayer said.

"And you're not gonna today. You really think she's at home?"

"She should be." Thayer pulled away from Corey's embrace
and linked their hands together. "How was she this morning?"

"A little rocky but I left her in Nora Warren's capable hands."
Corey led them up the stairs.

"She didn't leave with you?"

"Nora asked her to stay and she agreed."

"Huh, interesting," Thayer mused.

"Isn't it, though?"

The coffeehouse was busy but more subdued than usual.
Absent was the raucous laughter and loud conversation expected
at the end of the workday. Tables were full with no one shouting
to be heard.

"Weird." Corey looked around, glancing at Thayer with a
shrug as they made their way to the back.

Rachel wasn't at her table desk but curled up on the sofa,
eyes heavy lidded with her sock feet pressing into the hip of
Nora Warren. She was sitting at Rachel's feet working on her
laptop, a cup of coffee on the low table in front of her.

Corey shared a look with Thayer, who wore a matching expression of pleasant surprise. "Hey, girls," Corey greeted them.

"Hi, you two." Nora closed her laptop.

"Hey, dude." Rachel smiled crookedly and held out a loose fist for Corey to bump before rolling her eyes to Thayer. "Hey, gorgeous."

"Hey, yourself." Thayer knelt down in front of her and brushed her fingertips over her bruised eye with a wince. "You really should be at home, honey, but I'm glad to see you're not trying to be a hero and are taking it easy. May I?" She gestured to Rachel's side and at her nod of agreement, lifted her shirt to examine the bruising at her flank. "How do you feel?"

"Sore, but otherwise okay." She pushed herself up and swung her feet to the floor.

Thayer remained on her knees in front of her, suddenly looking uncertain and chewing her lip. "Listen, Rachel, now maybe isn't the best time, but I really need you to know how sorry I am—"

Rachel touched Thayer's lips with her fingertips, stopping her words. "Thayer, I swear to all that is good and holy, if you try to take responsibility for what happened to me last night I *will* think less of you."

"I just can't help thinking—"

"Can't hear you." Rachel slapped her hands over ears.

"Give it up, babe." Corey extended her hand to Thayer. "You think *I'm* stubborn."

Thayer sighed in frustration and took Corey's hand, letting her pull her to her feet. She looked down at Rachel. "Can I at least still worry about you a little?"

"You may, but I have been sufficiently supervised." Rachel's gaze flicked to Nora.

"I've been keeping an eye on her." Nora placed her laptop on the table and picked up her mug.

Corey dropped into an armchair across from them. "Have you been here all day?"

"I didn't have any appointments and my work is pretty portable. I can write a sermon anywhere and this place is positively vibrant and inspiring. I might have to become a regular."

Corey's gaze flicked to Rachel who was looking dopey from more than just medication.

"Did you get them to turn the volume down in here, too?" Thayer asked, taking the chair next to Corey.

"Not me," Nora said. "It was pretty obvious something was wrong when Rachel showed up. I think everyone is making an effort to be considerate and respectful."

Corey snorted a laugh. "Wow, Rach, what are you putting in the coffee? Your people love you."

Rachel smiled gingerly. "It's funny, right?"

"I think it's absolutely incredible," Nora said, and rested a hand on Rachel's leg. "And speaks volumes—no pun intended— to how highly you are regarded in the community."

"I agree." Thayer beamed at Rachel.

"Aw, y'all are gonna make me blush." Rachel ran a hand through her hair, making it stand up, and changed the subject. "What happened with the case today?"

"Collier positively identified the body and we have a cause of death," Corey said. "Can't tell you more than that, but the case is closed and the police won't need to speak to Jeremy again about it."

Nora exhaled slowly as if she had been holding her breath. "That's good. What about what happened to Rachel?"

"Nothing we can do about that at the moment, but Collier is still working on it. He's going to have a car drive by when it can to keep an eye on the house."

"Those goddamn little shit-for-brains," Rachel muttered. Her gaze flicked to Nora. "Sorry."

"Rachel, you don't need to apologize to me for every profanity. I've heard it all and said it all. I had to train myself to speak less colorfully when expressing my displeasure—or pleasure, for that matter. I promise you, I will not be offended nor will I think less of you for your creative use of explicatives. I find you irresistibly charming just the way you are."

Rachel gaped at her. "You do?"

A flush crept up Nora's face. "Well, I…"

Before she could speak a throat cleared nearby. "Hello, Nora."

"Lisa!" Nora blurted and sat bolt up spilling her coffee onto the floor. "Oh, shit..." she hissed and dropped a few napkins on the floor to soak up the mess.

Corey glanced at the woman interrupting them—small and pale like a stiff wind could blow her away at any moment. She had large, red-rimmed and anxious eyes, and brown hair in a sagging bun.

"I got it." Corey scooted around the table and mopped up the mess before Rachel tried to.

Nora set her cup down. "What are you...Are you okay?"

Lisa smiled wanly. "I'm sorry to just drop in on you like this, but I really wanted to talk to you and the parish secretary said I may be able to find you here."

"Of course, whatever you need." Nora looked around at the others apologetically. "If you'll excuse me I have to—"

"You don't have to do anything," Lisa said and looked like she could disappear inside herself at any moment. "I don't really know how I thought this was going to work."

Corey's gaze flicked to Thayer who was eyeing Lisa with concern.

"Why don't you sit down." Thayer stood and guided her into the chair Corey had vacated.

She sat like her strings had been cut. "Thank you. I'm sorry to interrupt your gathering. I'm Lisa Bright."

Thayer sucked in an audible breath and Rachel sat up sharply with a wince.

"Yes, Marcus Bright's wife...widow," she said wearily and hiccupped a breath. "Please, don't let that scare you away. I, um, find being around people helps."

From her crouch on the floor Corey stared at her. Two days ago she'd seen the body of her husband, head blown open, naked and disemboweled. She looked away. She could feel the heat rising in her cheeks. It felt a bit like guilt, as if she'd done something wrong and Lisa could read her mind. She wiped furiously at the spill that had already been cleaned up.

Lisa Bright couldn't read her mind but Thayer clearly could. Her hand came down gently on her shoulder. "Sweetheart, can you go up front for us, please. Maybe some tea for Lisa and Rachel and coffee for me and Nora?"

She jumped to her feet with a grateful look to Thayer. "Be right back."

"I'll come, too." Rachel stood carefully. Only the tightness around her eyes gave away her discomfort which Corey knew had as much to do with not knowing how to be around Lisa Bright than any physical pain she was still feeling.

CHAPTER TWENTY-SEVEN

"Well, this is awkward," Corey muttered as she leaned against the counter after giving Lainey their order.

"I feel like I'm in the fucking twilight zone," Rachel said.

"I held her dead husband's heart in my hand. What's your excuse?"

"I suck at compassionate words?"

"No, you don't."

"I do today."

"Me too," Collier said from behind them and slurped his coffee loudly. "Hope you weren't looking for any—tapped out."

Corey jumped. "Jesus, man, lurk much?"

Rachel scowled. "If you came to tell me I don't have a case against those guys unless I can identify them, don't bother."

"Take it easy, Wiley, I'm not done yet."

"What are you doing here then?" Corey asked.

He raised his cup. "Gettin' coffee. I'm about to head down to the Towne Plaza and talk to some of the shop owners and I needed a fix. Warren hasn't been able to find any record of complaints against those guys for loitering or anything. You said you knew the guys from the bowling alley had called the cops?"

"That's what they told me," Rachel said.

"Speaking of Warren…" He stared in the direction of the sofa and chairs. "Tell me that's not who I think it is with Doc and the Reverend?"

Corey's gaze flicked to Rachel who shrugged one shoulder. "Lisa Bright."

"What's she doing here?"

Corey smiled grimly. "Don't look at us. She goes to the UU church and showed up looking for Nora. We didn't even wait around long enough to find out why. Could just be something about funeral arrangements."

"Here you go, Corey," Lainey interrupted them to pass a tray filled with coffee, tea and pastries across the counter. "Now, please leave so I can serve paying customers."

"Thanks, Lainey." Corey held the tray and stared at her destination.

"Problem?" Collier asked.

"I'm such a coward. I just can't…" Corey scrunched up her face. "I weighed what was left of his brain, you know?"

"Tell you what," he said. "You let me tag along for a few minutes and find out what's up with Lisa Bright and I'll tag *you* out and ask you come to the plaza with me."

Corey's eyes slid closed with relief. "Oh, god bless you."

"Hey, I hope this is to everyone's liking." Corey set the tray down and gestured to Collier. "And I found—"

"You called the cops?" Lisa Bright sat up in her chair, eyes darting around nervously.

Thayer and Nora looked confused.

"No, Mrs. Bright, no one called me." Collier came around to where she could see him better. "I stop here often for coffee and I came to check on Ms. Wiley"—he gestured to Rachel—"who was injured last night. I saw you and I wanted to come pay my respects."

Lisa's pale complexion reddened with embarrassment before draining of color again. "I apologize," she mumbled and picked up a mug of tea with a trembling hand. "I'm a little on edge."

"Totally understandable," he said calmly. "I know this is a terrible time for you. Is there anything I personally, or the police in general, can do for you or your family?"

Lisa shook her head and stared into her mug.

"Lisa," Nora said gently. "May I tell Sergeant Collier what you were just sharing with us?"

"It doesn't matter," she murmured. "It won't change anything."

Though her answer was somewhat vague Nora apparently interpreted it as permission to share. "Lisa has just been telling us about how much stress Marcus's job had been causing him of late."

Collier nodded. "He was a good man. He worked hard on behalf of the city and would have made a terrific mayor."

Lisa's shoulders began to shake and she mumbled something toward the ground.

Collier's eyes flicked around and Corey saw the same look of confusion on everyone's face. "I beg your pardon?" he said.

Lisa raised her head, tears flowing again. "He never wanted to be mayor." She hiccupped a breath. "He had been approached for the last three years about challenging the Republican incumbent, but he never wanted it. Maybe when the boys were older, he would always say."

"What changed his mind?" Collier asked.

She shook her head. "I don't know. Nothing. I was as surprised as anyone else when he announced his candidacy. Then there were late nights and phone calls he had to take privately and his bleak moods."

"And you don't have any idea what caused the change in his mood?" Collier asked.

She sobbed a breath, scrubbing her face with her hands. "He didn't talk about it, but from what little bits I overheard, it had something to do with a real estate deal. I heard snatches of conversations about property values and tenants."

"Apartments?" Nora asked.

Lisa shrugged helplessly.

"But you think whatever it was had something to do with his...death?" Nora clarified.

Lisa's eyes cleared for the first time and her voice grew strong. "I'm certain of it."

Corey chewed the tip of her thumb and stared out the passenger window of Collier's unmarked car. She'd been in it before a few times—often in the back. It wasn't a far drive from Rachel's shop to the Towne Plaza. "What did you think about all that?" she finally asked.

Collier had grown distant. "Who knows. She's right about one thing, though."

"What?"

"It doesn't change anything."

"Well, sure, yeah, he's still dead by suicide. But if something was stressing him out, or you know, if he were triggered by something, wouldn't you want to know? If you were his wife? I mean, if someone I loved killed themselves…" She shuddered. "You better believe I'd be finding out why. Or getting someone else to."

He glanced at her as he pulled into the plaza which was still bustling with after-Christmas shoppers. "And you'd like me to do what about it, exactly?"

Corey sighed. "Nothing, I guess. It just sucks."

"I'll be back in a few." He parked as close to the bowling alley as he could.

"I'm coming, too."

"I'd rather you didn't."

"Shoulda stuck me in the back, then." She threw the door open and strode toward the bowling alley leaving Collier to catch up. She slowed only long enough to glance around for any black-clad assailants she recognized.

"They're probably laying low." He gripped the door over her shoulder. "Remember they just found out their buddy died this morning."

"Sure they did."

Collier flashed his badge at the shoe rental desk and spoke loudly enough to be heard over the thundering rumble of ten-pin. "Sergeant Collier here to see the owners, Gary or Mark Miles."

The surprised young man gaped at him a moment before scampering away into a back room.

"I'm Gary Miles," a tall lanky forty-something man said less than a minute later. "What can I do for you?"

"Sergeant Collier," he said. His gaze flicked to Corey. "And my associate."

Gary Miles nodded. "This about the body?"

Collier flipped open his notebook, pen poised, and got right to it. "I want to know about the complaints you supposedly made to the police about a group of kids—"

His expression darkened. "Supposedly? We must have called you guys half a dozen times in the last few months. It's gotten so bad we've had complaints from parents. Parties are cancelling and we're losing daily business. And we're not the only ones. This is far from the poshest shopping area, but those little bastards are killing business and bringing the whole area down. They're like a crack house in your neighborhood."

"I've found no record of charges against anyone for disturbances at this location," Collier said evenly.

Gary Miles's face reddened and pinched, clearly trying to keep himself under control in front of the police. "That's bullshit. Check your dispatch records. The same officer showed up every damn time. He even carted a few of them away at least once."

Corey's gaze darted between Collier and Gary Miles who had worked himself up into quite a froth. Collier's eye was starting to twitch like it did when he got angry. She wondered if it was this guy he was angry at or something else.

He flipped his notebook closed and tucked it into his pocket slowly like he was giving himself a minute. "Do you know the name of the—"

"Yeah. Taggart."

CHAPTER TWENTY-EIGHT

It was a tense ride back to the Old Bridge Coffee House. Corey had so many questions. She bit down on the inside her of cheek to keep from asking them and getting herself in trouble when Collier was clearly seething—at least while the car was moving. His face was tight and his eye twitched madly.

He whipped into a spot in front, but she made no move to get out. "What?" he barked.

"If Taggart picked up those kids why isn't there a record of their arrest?"

"There would be if he had actually arrested them."

"He didn't arrest them? Why not? Is he covering for them?" Her mind whirled with this new piece of information.

He didn't reply and stared furiously out the windshield.

"He could have known who that kid was the entire time he was in the morgue this morning. He could have known the sister. He didn't say anything to you?"

"No, he did not. Now, get out. I have work to do."

Corey scrambled out of the car, but paused closing the door. "What should I tell everyone?"

"Tell them I'm handling it." He pulled away with the door still open forcing Corey to jump back out of the way and slam it closed.

Everyone was where she had left them when Corey walked back to the sofa, with the exception of Lisa Bright who was nowhere to been seen. The coffee and plates with muffin crumbs had been cleared away and replaced with wine glasses and a tray of sandwiches.

Corey flopped into the available armchair with a tremendous sigh and closed her eyes. "What time is it?"

"Almost seven," Thayer said. "You've been gone less than an hour."

"Why?" Rachel asked.

Corey sat up and perused the coffee table. "It just feels way later. Is there a drink for me?"

Nora was lounging back against the sofa. One hand clutched around her near empty wine glass and the other arm flung out across the back of the sofa such that one slight shift would bring her arm across Rachel's shoulders. She either wasn't much of a drinker or that wasn't her first glass. She pointed to a full glass with her foot. "That one is yours."

"You okay?" Thayer reached across the space between the chairs.

Corey took her hand, lacing their fingers together. "Yeah, just another piece of the puzzle I can't quite fit."

"You gonna share?" Rachel asked.

"Collier asked the owner of the bowling alley about the calls he had made to the police about that gang—or whatever we're calling them—and told him there was no record of any arrests. The guy went off, saying he had called the police a bunch of times. I thought he was going to have a stroke he was so pissed. Anyway, turns out when he made the calls the same officer showed up every time."

"Who?" the three said in unison.

Corey sat forward, brows raised dramatically. "Taggart."

Nora, Rachel and Thayer all looked at each other then back at her with varying degrees of confusion.

"Who's that?" Thayer finally asked.

"Taggart. I just ran into him right outside the night of the Christmas party, but I first met him as that stupid fucking idiot who was there when…" Corey trailed off, realizing she knew him from the Crandall investigation. He had been in their house being a total pig and Collier had torn strips off him. Bringing any of that up was not a good idea. "You know what? You don't know him. I was the only one…never mind."

"Moving on." Rachel gestured for Corey to get on with the story. "What about him?"

"I guess he responded to all the complaint calls," she said.

"And?" Thayer prodded.

"And there's no record of an arrest."

Nora frowned. "Maybe he never caught up with them?"

Corey shook her head. "The bowling alley owner said he saw him cuffing and stuffing them on at least one occasion."

"So…" Rachel drawled. "What? Help out my drug-addled brain."

"I think he was in on it," Corey stated and sat back, taking a slug of her wine.

"In on *what*, exactly?" Thayer asked.

Nora pursed her lips. "In on some nefarious plot to harass the good people of the Towne Plaza? Please, do explain."

Rachel barked a laugh. "You're such a keeper, Nora."

She smiled. "I'm glad you think so."

Corey scowled and drummed her fingers on her wine glass. "Maybe it's all a plot to lower the property value. Apparently this gang is causing enough trouble that businesses are suffering."

"Orchestrated by whom?" Thayer asked.

"The buyer." Corey sat forward again. "Or their agent."

Rachel pursed her lips. "Real estate agent?"

"No. Just a general bad actor working on behalf of the…You know what? Forget it, but I mean, think about it."

Rachel released a loud breath and sagged against the sofa. "You make no sense and I can't think about this anymore. I feel like my head is going to explode."

Corey kept her expression carefully neutral when she saw Nora finally make that shift, lowering her hand to brush an errant tuft of Rachel's spiky hair behind her ear. "You feel okay?" she asked softly.

Rachel stilled at the brief, but intimate touch. "Yeah," she squeaked and cleared her throat. "Just tired."

Corey dared a glance at Thayer who hadn't missed a thing, a smile hinting at her lips. "We should get going," Thayer said.

"Yeah," Corey agreed.

Their goodbyes were interrupted when Nora's phone vibrated around the table with a text. "Excuse me."

"You need anything before we go?" Corey asked Rachel.

"No, I'm good. I'll call you—"

"Oh, no," Nora blurted, her hand over her mouth as she stared at her phone.

Thayer sat up. "What's wrong?"

"I'm sorry." Nora surged to her feet. "I'm sorry. I have to go."

"Whoa, whoa, whoa." Rachel lurched forward and grabbed her wrist. "Nora, what's going on?"

"It's Jeremy." She held up her phone with a trembling hand. "He's going to the plaza and he asked me to call Kelly. I think he's going to challenge those boys—get them to try and hurt him."

Corey jumped to her feet. "Call Kelly first then try Jeremy and keep trying him. Thayer, call Collier. I'll drive."

CHAPTER TWENTY-NINE

"I don't know, Kelly. I wasn't looking at the time. Not long—seven minutes ago, maybe," Nora snapped into the phone. "I've tried. He's not answering. I don't know. We're almost there. No, I'm not waiting for you. Just get there, Kelly, please."

Corey glanced in the rearview to see Nora hunched over, elbows on her knees, hands clasped in front of her face and her eyes closed. Rachel was watching her worriedly, her hand hovering over her back, but not touching her.

She couldn't spare them another glance as she approached the plaza and slowed, turning into the parking lot. It was even busier now than an hour ago with last-minute errand runners before the New Year's long weekend. It was full dark, and the oncoming lights, bundled shoppers and flurries beginning to fall were making it difficult to see anything clearly.

"Sit tight. I'm just going to drive by from one end to the other and see if we can find him." Corey merged into the line of cars poking past the storefronts, stopping every fifteen yards for pedestrians and turning cars.

Thayer peered through the windshield. "I can't see anything. There are too many people."

"I don't like this," Nora said.

"The police will be here any minute," Rachel said.

"This is too slow." Nora flung open the door the next time Corey came to a stop.

"Nora, wait damn it!" Rachel shouted after her, but she was already gone. "Fuck!"

"Shit, shit shit." Corey twisted around in her seat but wasn't able to track her and keep her eyes on the traffic. They were stuck between two rows, neither able to move forward or back. "Thayer?"

Thayer unbuckled her belt. "I'll go. Catch up to us."

Corey gripped her arm and held her gaze with a worried look, wanting more than anything to tell her not go, that it was too dangerous. "Please, be careful."

"I will." She squeezed Corey's leg briefly and was gone, jogging to catch up with Nora.

Thayer panted from more than just exertion and cold. She was scared—irrationally so. There were hundreds of people around. Corey was within shouting distance and the police were on the way, yet her legs felt ready to give beneath her and her heart thundered in her chest as she ran to where Nora had slowed near the bowling alley.

"They've gotta be around here somewhere." Nora's breath came out in panicked puffs as she crossed the front of the bowling alley, her face lit up eerily from the flashing colored lights from within.

"They won't be out in the open," Thayer gasped, sounding winded enough to catch Nora's attention.

She frowned at her. "Are you all right? You look really—"

"I'm fine." Thayer peered around the corner to a narrow walkway. "Down here."

Nora headed down the walkway, slowly at first then picking up speed, walking quickly through the poorly cleared, ankle-deep slush. If there was any noise giving away Jeremy's location,

Thayer couldn't hear it over the sound of her own breathing as she followed Nora away from the safety of the lights and people.

Thayer pulled her phone to text Corey and immediately jammed it back into her pocket when Nora yelled, "Jeremy!" And burst out the back of the walkway at a dead run.

Thayer caught a flash of movement and the sounds of a chase. She hesitated for only a moment before sucking in a deep breath and running after them.

"Let me out, Corey," Rachel demanded when they moved again.

"Just hang on. Let me park." Corey whipped down the first available row as soon as she could. "Can you see them?"

"No." Rachel hopped out of the car before it even stopped. "They were heading toward the bowling alley."

"Let's start there." Corey trotted toward that end of the plaza with Rachel struggling to keep up.

Corey stood in front of the bowling alley, the sidewalk lit with the flashing lights from within and the loud rock music drifting to the outside. The snow started to fall harder and she looked up and down the covered sidewalk peering around the people hurrying in and out of stores. "Shit."

Rachel headed toward the drugstore, her head whipping back and forth looking for any sign of them. "Oh shit." She stopped, looking toward the buildings. "Corey, there's an access way between the buildings."

Corey jogged over and peered down the dark walkway with a weak light over a side entrance to the bowling alley on the right. "Come on."

As soon as they stepped between the buildings, the traffic noise lessened and sound of the music was reduced to a throbbing bass, which lent an ominous soundtrack to the darkening walk toward the back of the plaza.

"Hear anything?" Rachel asked.

"I don't know." She paused and pulled her phone.

"What are you doing?"

"Texting Kelly." Corey fired off a quick text and jammed the phone back in her pocket while they worked their way down the walk. As they neared the end, the sounds of angry shouting, muffled by the snow, could be heard.

"Get that murdering little faggot!"

"I got him. Fucking queer little bitch is trying to hide."

They heard a thump and crash against a dumpster, running feet and unintelligible shouts.

"Jeremy, don't stop. What are you doing?"

"Stay out of this bitch unless you wanna get hurt!"

"The police are on the way!"

Corey and Rachel burst into the back of the plaza to see the looming shapes of dumpsters, lining the rear access road partially lit by security lights high on the walls over back entrances to the shops. Beyond the dumpsters was the snowy hill leading up to the city cemetery. Corey paused again turning both right and left.

"There!" Rachel pointed to the shadows of running figures, flashing dully in and out of the overhead lights. They took off after them, the only sound feet pounding through slush and labored breathing.

"Stand up, faggot!" one of the boys yelled followed by the sound of scuffling and bodies thumping and a shout of pain.

"Hit him again!"

"Get off him!" Nora cried.

"Someone shut that bitch up!"

"No. Stop!" Thayer shouted.

Corey skidded to a stop between two dumpsters, her heart hammering and breath billowing out in frosty clouds. "Thayer?"

"Here, Corey," Thayer gasped, standing with her arms outstretched between a down and injured Jeremy with Nora crouched over him, protecting him with her body against the three boys, their black hoods pulled up and fists raised.

"Back off." Corey advanced on them, straightening to her full height and widening her stance, this time ready for a fight. "Now!"

The night lit up with red and blue flashing lights and a whoop of the siren as a patrol car pulled into the access road.

Rachel caught up to them, skidding on her knees next to Jeremy and Nora.

"Fuck!"

"Go! Go!"

Corey moved first and fast, slamming her hands into the back of the nearest boy as he turned to run, sending him sprawling into the slush and sliding several yards on his face.

A second boy was making a move to scramble up the hill when she caught up with him, grabbing his ankle. "You little piece of shit," she snarled, yanking his leg viciously, dragging him back to the ground.

"Police! Don't move." Kelly pounded down the road, flashlight out, pinning the last boy with the light, one hand on his weapon ready to draw it if necessary. "Down on the ground, now. Arms out in front of you. Do it, now!"

All three lay spread eagle in the snow, breathing heavily and whimpering.

"Don't shoot."

"We didn't do nothin'."

"My mom's a lawyer."

"Shut up!" Kelly barked, kneeling next to the first boy and jerking his arms behind his back, securing them with plastic cuffs before he moved toward the next. "Is everyone all right?"

"Thayer?" Corey said, turning to her.

"I'm fine."

"Jeremy's hurt," Nora called.

"Let me see." Thayer knelt on the ground next to him, gently turning his face toward the light showing a split lip, dripping blood and a welt under his eye. She pulled a pack of tissues from her pocket and wiped gently at the blood. "Looks like you took a pretty good shot, but it doesn't look too bad."

"No?" Jeremy asked wide eyed.

"No," Thayer smiled reassuringly. "Are you hurt anywhere else?"

"No." He shook his head. "I'm fine. Did we get 'em?"

"Jeremy." Nora huffed an angry breath. "Why would you do this? What were you thinking?"

"I was thinking I couldn't let these losers keep beating up on people, Nora. What if it had been one of the younger guys? What if it had been you? What if they had come to the house or the church? We could have lost everything."

"I could have lost you!" Nora's eyes filled with tears.

"You didn't. You won't," he said softly.

"God help me, Jeremy, if you ever pull something like this again…" She trailed off, head hanging, tears spilling over.

"I'm sorry I scared you, Nora." Jeremy scooted over in the snow and wrapped his arms around her.

She returned his embrace, pulling him in fiercely.

"Thayer?" Corey placed a hand on her shoulder.

"I'm good." Thayer covered Corey's hand with her own and let Corey pull her to her feet.

"Rach?" Corey turned to her.

She was sitting with her back against the dumpster, legs drawn up and arms resting across her knees. "Fucking hurts to breathe."

"No shit. Come on, get out of the snow." Corey reached for her hands and lifted her to her feet. "You okay?"

"Yep." Rachel took a step, grimacing. "How do I look?"

"Hot."

They made their way over to Kelly as he was loading the last of the kids into the back of his car and Mirandizing them. It was a tight fit with all three of them back there. Then one of them started to cry.

"What now?" Corey asked, her arm around Thayer and Thayer's finger laced with the hand draped over her shoulder.

"Now, I run these assholes downtown and book them on assault charges. Once I get them processed, I'll get forensics to run any trace evidence on their clothes and see if we can link them to the attack on Rachel." He slammed the door on them. "I need statements and Jeremy needs to get checked out by a doctor and we need photos."

"You need all this tonight?" Rachel asked, visibly wilting after the physical exertion.

"I need Jeremy to get looked at tonight and a statement from him, and whichever of you witnessed what happened."

"I'll take him over to the ED and get Watson to see him. He's on tonight," Thayer said. "We can come to the station after."

"I'll go with you," Nora said.

Rachel straightened as well as she could. "I'll come—"

"Home with me," Corey finished for her. "No arguments. You look like hell. We can give our statements in the morning if they need more."

The sound of another car drew everyone's attention and Collier stepped out, heading toward them. "Everyone all right?" he asked as he strode toward them, his gaze taking in each of them in turn.

Kelly straightened under the assessing gaze of his superior. "Jeremy's a little banged up, Sarge. Thayer and Nora are taking him to the hospital." He gestured to his full patrol car. "I'm going to process these clowns."

Collier nodded sharply and eyed Jeremy. "Why don't you ride with me, son? Doc and the reverend, too."

Corey grabbed Thayer's hand before she could follow them and pulled her into a hard embrace, burying her face into her hair and breathing her in. "You were kind of a badass," she whispered, squeezing her tightly.

Thayer laughed a little hysterically and squeezed her back just as hard. "Just *kind of*?"

Corey pulled away and met her gaze, brushing her windblown hair from her face. "I'll wait up."

"You better."

CHAPTER THIRTY

When they met up at the police station after the hospital, Jim led Thayer and Nora to a small interview room. He directed an officer to get them coffee, water or whatever they needed, before leading Jeremy away to take his statement. They had been there an hour already and it was nearing nine. There was nothing wrong with the temperature in the police station, yet Thayer still felt chilled and hadn't removed her coat.

She became aware her level of tension was unsustainable when her hand, seemingly of its own accord, clenched and crushed her empty foam coffee cup with a pop, startling her.

Nora looked up from her phone. "You okay?" She had spent the time texting furiously, the guys at AllWays House, Thayer assumed.

"Sorry," Thayer whispered. She took a deep breath and shrugged out of her coat and placed her hands flat on the table, straightening up in her chair. She set her tongue just behind her teeth and breathed in deeply through her nose to a slow count of four. She closed her eyes and held the breath before exhaling slowly through her mouth. It took several long minutes before she felt the tension ease from her chest, her heart rate slow and her shoulders relax.

"You're intentional breathing," Nora said softly.

"Yes," Thayer said, keeping her eyes closed and continuing the technique. "It helps."

"The work you do must be very stressful."

Thayer went through another round of breathing before responding. "My job used to be the most stressful part of my life."

"Do you want to talk about it?"

Thayer breathed in, holding it before exhaling and opening her eyes. "Did Kelly tell you how we met?"

"No, I guess not. I assumed through your work or Corey's."

"True to a degree." Thayer smiled slightly. "You know about the police breaking up a drug ring at the end of the summer?"

Nora nodded. "Kelly was very proud of his involvement in that case. His first undercover assignment…"

Thayer nodded, seeing Nora's expression turn from surprise to understanding. "And he stayed overnight in his patrol car parked outside my house so I would feel safe."

"Oh, Thayer, I'm so sorry." Nora reached across the table and covered Thayer's hands with her own. "Thank you, for everything you've done for me and for Jeremy. It must have been so…challenging for you after everything you've been through."

"Challenging, yes." She smiled wistfully. "I'm beginning to think maybe in some good ways."

"How so?"

Thayer sat back, steepling her hands in front of her face, and let out a long breath. "I, um, think I've been holding onto this idea that none of the things—the bad things—that have happened to me would've happened were it not for my involvement with Corey."

"None of the good things either, I assume?"

"That's right. But I said it out loud to her the other night, before I even met you. I blurted it out before I realized what I was saying—that part of me blames her for the trouble we've had and yet…"

Nora raised her brows. "Yet?"

Thayer laughed out loud and threw her arms out to the side. "Here I sit in the police station—again. And Corey is at home curled up with the puppy in front of the fire having drinks with her bestie. And Rachel, oh god, she doesn't have anything to do with any of this, and she was the one who suffered the most. Corey even did her best to talk me out of getting involved and I just steamrolled right over her because…because I…"

"You what?"

"I needed this, I think. I needed to help. I needed a win." She laughed softly. "And I definitely need to let go of the idea that Corey is the root of all our drama. It's holding me back from her and it's not fair, and quite clearly, not true."

Nora smiled. "You know there's a women's group that meets at the church every couple of weeks for survivors."

"Thank you, Nora, but I think I'm doing okay."

"I think you are, too, which was why I was thinking maybe you could come in and speak to some of the women who maybe aren't as far along as you. Maybe share your story?"

Her lips parted in surprise. "Um, okay. I could do that, I guess. If you think it would help."

Nora smiled. "I do think it would help."

"Thayer," Steph Austin said from the doorway.

"Steph." Thayer stood abruptly at the sight of her friend and moved around the table.

Steph pulled her into a strong embrace. "Are you all right? Jim filled me in."

"I'm fine." She stepped away, swiping at tears threatening.

Steph grinned. "I gotta say I almost didn't recognize you here without Corey."

"Ha, yeah." Thayer gestured to Nora. "I have a new partner in crime today. Reverend Nora Warren this is Detective Steph Austin."

"Kelly's sister, of course." Steph extended her hand. "Very pleased to meet you. I'm sorry you've been stuck here so long. I know it's not very comfortable."

Nora shrugged and tapped against the hard plastic chair. "Eh, not so bad. Better than most church pews."

"Or ED waiting room chairs," Thayer added.

"Good to know," Steph said dryly. "I'll remember this when we're talking over drinks about which of our chosen institutions is most disappointing."

Thayer gasped. "Are you suggesting there are flaws in the healthcare system, Steph?"

"Or that organized religion isn't completely benevolent?" Nora added with feigned indignation.

Steph's smile at the lighthearted moment faltered.

"What's wrong?" Thayer asked feeling the tension rise again in her chest.

"We've discovered this case—the assault against Jeremy Landis and Rachel—is bigger and far more complex than originally thought. Throw a corrupt officer into the mix and it's a mess."

Thayer's gaze was drawn past Steph's shoulder to a striking woman in an expertly tailored, black pinstripe pantsuit being escorted through the station by Jim Collier. She looked to be in her early forties with long, dark hair. She was flawlessly made up, manicured, and accessorized in gold and she exuded power.

The woman turned toward them as if she could feel Thayer's eyes on her from across the room. She boldly assessed Thayer as she glided past without missing a step. Her lip curled into a seductive smile and was gone again so fast Thayer may have imagined it. "Who is that?" she asked.

"Come back and sit down and I'll tell you what I can," Steph said.

A loud pop of the crackling fire worked its way into Corey's unconscious after sleep had overtaken her, following a couple of beers with Rachel while she waited for Thayer to come home. She blinked her eyes open to see Thayer sitting cross-legged nearby on the bearskin rug, a glass of wine in one hand and her head resting in the other.

"Babe?" Corey pushed herself onto an elbow. "How long have you been home?"

"Hi." Thayer lifted her head. "Just long enough to shower, change and pour a glass."

"What time is it?"

"Close to midnight."

"Shit." Corey rubbed her eyes. "Aren't you tired?"

"I am…" Thayer sighed deeply, "…utterly exhausted but I need to unwind."

"Where is everyone else now?" Corey sat up all the way, crossing her legs.

"Kelly dropped Nora and Jeremy back at AllWays House and Steph gave me a lift home."

"Where the hell was Collier?"

"I'll get to that. I have a lot to tell you. How's Rachel?"

"Good. I got her sorted with food, a shower, and clean clothes and she's sleeping it off in the guest room with Charlie."

"Speaking of Charlie…" Thayer eyed the house. "Why is it so picked up in here? Did you vacuum? And where are the throw pillows?"

"Oh, um, that." Corey smiled sheepishly. "We were gone a really long time today. I think she must have gone over the gate again."

Thayer sighed dramatically. "Rest in peace, throw pillows. Anything else?"

"Your black heels," Corey mumbled and hopped up to head for the kitchen to get a beer. "Can I get you more wine?"

"Which black heels?"

"The sexy ones with the strap—"

"My slingbacks? Damn it, Corey, I was going to wear those to the party."

Corey came back around with her beer. "I'm sorry, babe. I'll do better with her, I promise."

"It's all right. She's not just your responsibility. We both need to do better and it gives me an excuse to shop, I guess. And you, moneybags, can pay. Now that the truth is out about which of us is rich, you can start replacing some items in my wardrobe that haven't held up under your, ahem, enthusiastic affection."

"Can I at least pick out—"

"Under no circumstances." Thayer's smile faded and she patted the rug next to her. "Come back and sit down."

Corey lowered herself next to her. "How's Jeremy doing?"

"Surprisingly well and quite pleased with himself actually, much to Nora's frustration. His injuries were minor."

"And those little ass—"

"The boys have lawyers, of course. The good news is they won't be arraigned until after the new year so they'll be cooling their heels in jail for a few days. They were all in tears by the time Jim informed them their friend would still have likely been alive and they could have helped him. It was kind of sad, actually."

"What about the sister? Did they arrest her, too?"

"Yes, but it's complicated."

Corey sucked on her beer. "Hit me. I can take it."

Thayer took a long swallow of her wine and blew out a harsh breath. "Those kids were being paid to cause trouble at the Towne Plaza."

Corey blinked. "Why? By who?"

"As much as it pains me to say it, you were right," Thayer smiled grimly. "It was a long game to try and bring down the property value. They were never supposed to get into too much trouble and have anyone look too closely into what was going on."

"Jesus," Corey breathed. "Who's behind it?"

"Well, Jim's still working all that out, but the next level up—their handler—was Officer Taggart, I guess."

"No shit. That fucker."

"Yeah. He's been the one protecting the kids from arrest. Making sure he got the calls and never filing a report or putting them into the system."

"He's going to jail," Corey sneered.

"Actually, I don't know about that. It goes way beyond him and he's cutting a deal as we speak. He was on the payroll of a guy named Paolo Costa."

"Who the hell is that? Sounds ultra-shady."

"He is, it seems. He runs a money lending operation called SwiftLend."

"Seriously? Sounds like a movie mobster."

"Oh, there's more. Turns out that's just his side hustle and he's a junior partner at Tagliotti, Mancini and Castiglione."

Corey choked on her beer. "No way. They are mob. I fucking knew it."

"I don't know about that and you won't catch me saying it too loud. Seems they're disavowing any knowledge of Costa's activities. I caught a glimpse of Carina Mancini at the station. She does not look like someone you want to cross. I strongly encourage you to drop that joke and let it go."

"No joke." Corey blew out a breath. "Anything else?"

Thayer sighed. "Marcus Bright."

"Oh no," Corey groaned.

"Yeah, it's not entirely clear how he was involved, but it seems he may have had a loan with SwiftLend, which put him under the thumb of Costa. He may have been being pressured into his mayoral candidacy, and there will be an investigation to see if everything he did as councilman was above board. The police need to go back to Lisa Bright and get access to some of their financials and figure out what's going on and how or if he was tied into what was happening at the Towne Plaza. It's going to be huge stain on the city and Jim described at as 'a big shit sandwich and everyone's taking a bite'."

"Aw, that sucks." Corey scrubbed her face. "I'm sorry."

"Yeah, me too," Thayer agreed. "Nora has offered to help her out and I really can't think of anyone better. Lisa Bright is going to have a tough time."

"I really like Nora," Corey said. "And Jeremy."

"Yeah, I do too, and I'd like to see more of them." Thayer set her wineglass aside and took Corey's beer from her before slipping her hand around the back of her neck. "Know who else I like?"

"Me?" Corey grinned.

"You." Thayer kissed her gently. "Will you go somewhere with me tomorrow morning?"

"Of course." Corey kissed her back. "But you know it's Sunday, right?"

Thayer smiled. "Exactly the point."

CHAPTER THIRTY-ONE

"Holy shit, dude!" Corey gaped at Rachel, looking her up and down. "Where did you get that?"

"Oh, this?" Rachel ran a hand down her red, Spiderman suit jacket with bright blue web accents, matching blue pants and blue tie on a white, button-down dress shirt. "Cool, huh? You jelly?"

"Oh, my god, yes." Corey continued to ogle her. She looked geek sharp.

"I'll send you the link." Rachel grinned, checking her out. "In the meantime, I have to say, you look smokin.'" Her gaze flicked to Thayer. "You do good work."

"What?" Corey looked down at herself in her black jeans, black silk T-shirt under a fitted, silver tuxedo jacket with black, silk collar and cuffs. "You don't think I can dress myself?"

"Not like this, you can't." Rachel nodded her approval then pushed Corey aside, eyes lighting up at Thayer in a silver-sequined, sleeveless maxi dress with choker collar and thigh high slit up the side. "But enough about you, dude." Rachel clasped Thayer's hands in her own and leaned in to give her a kiss. "You look stunning, Thayer."

"Thank you, Rachel. Your gallantry is always appreciated." Thayer beamed. "Happy New Year." She cocked her head and eyed Rachel's face, the bruises barely detectable. "Who did your makeup?"

"Jeremy. Wait 'til you get a load of the band's full glam makeup. Those guys are a fucking riot."

"How's Nora?" Corey asked.

Rachel's face fell. "I haven't see her yet. The guys said she got called away on an emergency with one of her flock but hopes to make it back before ten."

"You know she'll be here if she can." Corey smiled encouragingly. "If not, I'll kiss you at midnight."

"In your dreams," Rachel scoffed.

"Move it along up there, you train wrecks."

Corey whirled around to see Collier and Steph waiting to move farther in and greet Rachel. She gaped at his perfectly tailored, charcoal grey suit with violet tie and pocket square matching Steph's violet, one shoulder, A-line cocktail dress. "Wow!" Corey laughed and stepped out of the way for them to move forward. "Look at you. I'm going to go ahead and give Steph all the credit here."

"Yeah, yeah," Collier grumbled, bending down to kiss Thayer on the cheek. "Happy New Year, Doc."

"Happy New Year, Jim." Thayer smiled at him. "Steph, you look lovely."

"Hey, Thayer, Happy New Year." She moved around Collier and Corey to give Thayer a hug.

"Rachel." Steph held her at arm's length and looked her over. "You're looking none the worse for wear given your eventful week."

"Thank you, but I did have some help. Wait 'til you meet the band."

The effusive greetings continued around the doorway as more guests arrived. Dana and Kelly came together to the continued surprise of no one. Corey nodded her approval as they moved past them to the bar.

Jude Weatherly arrived with Angela, though they might as well have stayed home for all the socializing they did with anyone else. They only had eyes for each other. All the house staff were there to party.

Rachel had hired caterers who flitted in and out of the crowd with hot hors-d'oeuvres, beer, wine, champagne, trays of noisemakers and party hats. In addition, there was a very well-appointed standing buffet along the serving counter.

The remaining junior partners of Tagliotti, Mancini and Castiglione took up an entire table in the corner and were not holding back in their good time.

Corey nudged Rachel and nodded toward them. "You still think that group isn't connected? Why are they even here?"

Rachel grew uncharacteristically serious. "You think I should have un-invited them? I don't know how they're involved, but if they are who you think I'm better off not knowing and going about my day."

"I don't know, Rach."

"I do. Time to mingle," she said and headed off to greet more guests.

The folks from the chamber of commerce and women's business association milled around the buffet trying to find an opening through the handful of gym rats Rachel had included in the guest list who were decimating the food platters.

"You driving tonight?" Collier appeared next to Corey.

"Hell, no," Corey replied and waved down a drinks tray. "We Ubered."

"I still don't get why no one takes cabs anymore." Collier gratefully accepted the beer she offered him and sucked half of it down. "Thanks."

"I take it you're not driving either?"

"Austin's on the wagon." Collier finished the first beer and swapped it with a fresh one from a passing tray.

"She on medication?"

"No."

"A diet?"

"Nope."

"Training for a marathon?"

"Uh-uh."

Corey sucked in a breath. "Oh, my shit, Collier, no fucking way."

He met her gaze. "Was hoping if someone else knew maybe I could start to wrap my brain around the idea of being a father again at my age—and with a woman I've been with for only a few months. Christ, my kids are in their twenties."

"Holy fuck balls!" Corey shouted, earning her a scowl from Thayer and Steph and disapproving glances from people she didn't know. She lowered her voice. "Steph's pregnant? How? I mean, aren't you…I mean, didn't you use…um…how?"

"The usual way," Collier said and refreshed his beer again. "Supported by a failed vasectomy."

"Oh, shit." Corey slapped a hand over her mouth to smother an inappropriate laugh. "Are you…I mean, what are you going to…or is she going to…er, are we happy?"

"Jesus Christ, Curtis, get a hold of yourself. Even I handled the news better than that."

"Sorry. I just don't want to say the wrong thing."

"Congratulations is fine."

"Yeah?" Corey smiled hesitantly.

He paused a moment, his gaze seeking out Steph and grinning at her before he turned back to Corey and returned her smile. "Yeah."

"Fucking congratulations." She punched him in the arm. "Dad."

Corey glanced over to see Steph and Thayer staring at them curiously. Corey raised her bottle and gave a dramatic thumbs up from across the room, eliciting an equally as dramatic eye roll and head shake from Steph followed by an audible shriek from Thayer when she caught up on the news and threw her arms around Steph in response.

"Good evening, ladies and gentlemen." Rachel stood on the stage at the microphone in front of the full band set up, beaming at her guests. "Thank you all for coming tonight. It is so fun to see you all here and…" She threw her arms wide; strings of multicolored beads draped over her arm clacked at the motion. "...Happy New Year!"

"Happy New Year!" the room chorused.

She punctuated her greeting by throwing the strings of beads out toward the guests and laughed as many, well into their cups, dove and fought over them, the victors hanging them around their necks.

"I just have a few words before I introduce our entertainment for the night," she went on. "You are all here tonight because, like me, you care about making *this* shop, and *your* shop, and *your* city a welcoming, accessible, safe place for all members of the community. But especially for the BIPOC and LGBTQ communities and the otherwise marginalized."

The applause was loud and long.

"Thank you." She swallowed hard, emotion thickening her voice. "This is a mission near and dear to my heart, made even more so by coming to know, in the last week, some very special people." She stopped, her gaze drawn toward the door.

Corey turned to see Nora Warren come in, slightly out of breath and cheeks rosy from the cold. She stilled, halfway out of her coat when she realized Rachel was staring at her, and therefore, so was everyone else. "Sorry I'm late," she called to Rachel, eyes flashing merrily. "Carry on."

Rachel cleared her throat, a blush creeping up her cheeks. "I can't go into all the details but I was reminded recently how important it is, still and always, for those of us in positions to do so, to fight for our friends' and neighbors' human rights, equality, and truth. So that everyone in this city, and in all cities, can enjoy the same opportunities those of us with privilege take for granted. If I can do that, in some small measure, by being a voice in the community, then I will speak up every chance I get and I ask you all to do the same. The very fact that you are here tonight to support me and each other says that you share my passion in this."

A cheer went up again and Corey found herself having a hard time swallowing around the emotion clogging her throat. She swiped at her eyes and whistled her approval.

"So, enough about me," Rachel grinned. "It is my insane pleasure to introduce to you some new friends of mine—a group of amazing young people and their fearless leader—Nora Warren and the AllWays House band."

Corey's eyes widened when Jeremy hopped up on stage. He looked fabulous, hair artfully styled with teal and silver glitter eye shadow, and teal lips. The rest of the band, Declan on drums, Trey on keyboards and Leo on base were as skillfully if not quite as flamboyantly made up. They all wore jeans and button up shirts in various flashy colors.

"Hey there. Happy New Year," Jeremy grinned mischievously. "So happy to be here playing for you tonight."

Corey whistled again, starting off another round of cheers while they waited for Nora to join them.

"Here she comes." Jeremy smiled and held out his hand for Nora to step up to the stage.

She looked relaxed and happy and dressed to kill in an emerald green, sleeveless V-neck cocktail dress with lace overlay.

"Oh, gosh." Nora grinned shyly and brushed hair out of her face. "I'm sorry I'm late. Hey there." She waved to someone she knew. "It's really great to be here with you tonight and it's lovely to see so many familiar faces. I hope to get a chance to speak with all of you tonight. Thank you so much to Rachel Wiley for inviting us to play. It's a real honor to ring in the New Year with all of you. This past year, like all the years before it and like all the years to come, was filled with successes and failures, opportunities to forgive and be forgiven, moments of grief and moments of grace. I hope you'll all join me in acknowledging one of this city's biggest tragedies, which came just the other day with the loss of Marcus Bright. I know many of you were close to him and my heart goes out to you in your time of mourning."

The merry chatter in the room quieted and many eyes bright with joy and drink now glittered with sadness.

"Though I didn't know him well, I had the pleasure of meeting Marcus a few times and I was always touched by his generosity and passion. The most recent time was at the Pride Festival this past summer. He and his wife and kids were rocking out to our music. After our first set he and I got into a heated debate about our favorite singer-songwriters, and I don't know how many of you know this, but he swore by John Denver as the greatest that ever was and asked if we could play something for him."

Nora's gentle humor broke the tension and some laughed.

Nora selected an acoustic guitar from its stand and lifted the strap over her head, settling it across her shoulders and strumming a few chords. "I wished I could at the time, but we hadn't prepared anything like that, so I told him next time I saw him at one of our shows I would have something ready for him. I know he's with us here tonight, so I'm going to play something for not just him, but for those of us who loved him who he left behind. I don't know if John Denver was a religious man, but from knowing his songs, he was definitely a spiritual one. You all know this one. If you feel moved, sing it with me. This is 'Wild Montana Skies.'"

The band sat still and gave their full attention to Nora as she began to play, just her and the guitar, strumming it powerfully and passionately. When she added her voice, the whole room was rapt while she sang a moving tribute to a man beloved by the community.

When the last chord fell silent the room remained quiet until a voice called out, raising a glass. "To Marcus," they said into the silence.

"To Marcus," others echoed and the room slowly filled up with sounds of conversation and joy again.

Corey felt Thayer come up behind her, threading her fingers through Corey's. "Wow," Corey breathed. "I want her to sing at *my* funeral."

Thayer leaned her head against Corey's shoulder. "I was kind of thinking maybe she could sing at our *wedding* first."

Corey's gaze snapped to Thayer. "What?"

"Let's get the band involved now." Nora's voice drowned out Corey's exclamations of shock. "This one should get the booze flowing and the blood pumping. Going out to the Women's Business Association in the house tonight with a shout out to the Queen of Soul, Aretha Franklin, and Annie Lennox. This is 'Sisters are Doin' it for Themselves.'"

"I'm going to catch up with Dana." Thayer gave Corey a quick kiss and a sly smile and was gone through the crowd.

"Wait! Thayer!" Corey called after her. "What does that mean? Are we getting married?"

"What's up, dude?" Rachel came to join her.

"What?" Corey was looking over the top of the crowd.

Rachel snapped her fingers in Corey's face. "Corey, focus, right here."

"What?" Corey's head turned to Rachel. "Sorry, what were you saying?"

"Nothing, yet. I was going to ask you if you were having a good time."

Corey looked around at the party in full swing. The music was terrific and Jeremy and Nora had obviously performed together for a while and were well practiced, thoroughly enjoying their art. "Yeah, it's amazing."

"And Nora Warren?" Rachel asked shyly. "What do you think of her?"

Corey laughed. "You hardly ever ask for my opinion let alone twice in one week."

"I think this time is different," Rachel admitted. "It feels different."

"Different, good?"

"Different, terrifying. And good—great—and terrifying."

Corey studied her friend, a slow smile creeping across her face. "Up until I met Nora Warren I would've had a hard time naming a single person I thought was good enough for you. Someone who shared your passion and had the energy to keep up with you and who wouldn't take any of your shit along the way."

"And now?" Rachel asked hopefully.

"And now…" Corey shrugged. "I'm not sure you're good enough for her."

"You're such an asshole."

"You wouldn't have me any other way."

The last notes of The Jonas Brothers' "Sucker" faded out and Nora took a drink from the bottle of water on the stool nearby while the applause wound down. "Thank you, so much." She laughed when Corey whistled again. "So, I have a confession to make as the hour creeps closer to midnight. Earlier this week, I accidentally overheard part of a conversation I wasn't meant to hear and I really don't want to start off the new year with this weighty of a secret, so I'm going to confess my transgression through song. But first, I have a thank you gift for Rachel. Will you come up here, please, Rachel?"

Rachel's eyes widened and she looked at Corey. "What do I do?"

"Put your big girl Spiderman suit on and get your ass up there." Corey gave her a shove toward the stage.

"There she is." Nora smiled at her. "I haven't seen you all night. Dec, you have it?"

The drummer reached behind his stool and whipped out a silver gift bag with red and silver tissue paper poking out the top.

Nora spoke into the microphone for everyone to hear. "This is just a little something from me to Rachel to say thank you for having us, and though we haven't known each other long, thank you for being such a good friend. I look forward to us getting to know each other better."

Rachel pulled apart the tissue paper and peered into the bag, her eyes going wide. "Oh, shit." She covered her face with her hand and reddened furiously.

"Show us!" someone yelled from somewhere in the crowd.

Rachel pulled it out, letting the leopard print Snuggie fall to its full length.

"That looks cozy," someone shouted.

"Room for two in there?" someone cackled from the back.

Corey cracked up as, against all the laws of nature, Rachel reddened further.

"This next song is for you, Rachel." Nora smiled and winked and the band started playing Mary Lambert's, "She Keeps Me Warm."

The countdown was starting and Corey had no idea where Thayer had gotten to.

"Ten."

"Nine."

She saw Thayer across the room, looking for her, too. Rachel was on the stage with Nora, standing close. She caught a glimpse of Jude and Angela sneaking off toward the restrooms as she crossed the room, wending her way through the rowdy drunks and people shouting in each other's ears to be heard over the merriment. Out of the corner of her eye she saw Watson Gregory III, who she hadn't seen all night, looking dreamily at his date.

"Eight."

"Seven."

"Six."

She paused, briefly to watch Dana pressing Kelly Warren up against the glass windows at the front of the shop, clearly having jumped the countdown. Collier and Steph were dancing, slowly, to music only they could hear.

"Five."

"Four."

"Three."

Thayer, a sexy smile playing at her lips and her eyes flashing with love and desire, closed the last few steps between them. "I thought you weren't going to make it."

"Two."

"One."

"Happy New Year!" The room erupted in cheers, champagne corks popped and whizzed toward the ceiling, noisemakers screeched, confetti-blast explosions came from all directions.

Corey slipped her hand around the back of Thayer's neck, tangling her fingers through her hair and pressing their bodies close, feeling the heat of her and the arousing beat of her heart into her own chest. "Happy New Year, babe." Corey's lips just brushed across Thayer's.

"Happy New Year, sweetheart," Thayer murmured before eliminating all space between them in their first kiss of the New Year, one full of promise and adventure.

EPILOGUE

"Are you going to be sad to leave tomorrow?" Corey asked, twining their hands together as they walked slowly through the surf at sunset, the gentle lapping waves flowing across their bare feet and erasing their footprints behind them.

"Yes," Thayer answered. "Especially if it means I don't get to see you dressed like this for six more months." She turned and unabashedly raked her eyes over Corey in blue and pink board shorts sitting low on her hips with matching racer back sports bra showcasing her well-defined body and bright, full-sleeve tattoo.

"You get to see me in less than this whenever you want." Corey returned her appreciative glance and grinned at Thayer in the black bikini, a sheer, gold sarong tied around her hips, her smooth bronze skin darkened by a week in the sun and gold highlights in her hair brighter against her naturally auburn curls.

"I don't get to see you in a wetsuit and all your diving gear," Thayer commented.

"I didn't realize you wanted to."

"Neither did I. Somehow you manage to make everything sexy—scrubs, elf pajamas and wetsuits."

"Noted." Corey laughed.

"I've had a wonderful time." Thayer squeezed her hand. "Your parents are lovely hosts and it's been so fun getting to know them. I see so much of them in you—your sense of humor, your smile, your stubbornness. It's amazing, Corey Marie Curtis."

"I don't know why you find that so funny. You knew what my middle name is and everyone's middle name is Marie."

"What's funny is your mom dropping middle name bombs whenever she's exasperated with you, which is a lot in case you hadn't noticed."

"I apparently take after my father quite a bit, so they say. They really love you and are already bugging me about when we're going to come back."

Thayer smiled. "We'll put something else on the calendar again soon. Maybe I'll even request vacation this time so you don't need to strong arm my colleagues."

Corey rolled her eyes. "It wasn't even like that."

"I'm teasing you, sweetheart. And, however it was, I'm very grateful."

"I miss Charlie," Corey sighed.

"Are you kidding? Charlie is having the time of her life at the shop, treated like royalty by every customer that comes through the door. I bet Rachel's going to have some explaining to do when we get back and take her home. The customers will wonder where she's gone."

"I know." Corey frowned comically. "I think I'm worried she won't remember me and won't want to come home."

"I wouldn't worry about that when the trade off to staying with Rachel is no lake hikes and quick trips to the shrubbery at the back of the parking lot. Maybe we should get Rachel a puppy, something small and snorty, and then we can have puppy play dates."

"That's a good idea. Like a French bulldog."

"So, apropos of nothing, I couldn't help but notice you've been on your phone a lot the last couple of days," Thayer commented. "What's up?"

"I've been in touch with a realtor about the condo. I'm meeting her when we get back to go over the space. She can help me stage and let me know what I need to paint and fix so it shows well."

"Already?" Thayer turned to her.

"Why wait? Why keep paying for something I'm not using? Are you having second thoughts about all this?"

"No." Thayer shook her head. "No, of course not. I just want you to be sure."

"Babe, we've talked about this. I'm sure. In fact, I'm so sure I've been thinking maybe we should talk about a joint bank account."

"Really?" Thayer stated and was quiet a long time.

"What?" Corey frowned, pulling them to a stop and searching Thayer's eyes with concern. "Did I say something wrong? I mean if you think that idea sucks, fine, we don't have to."

Thayer fought a smile. "I'm not sure I want you to have access to all my wealth."

Corey laughed and wrapped her arms around Thayer's waist, pulling her close and ducking her head to nip and suck at her neck. "You mean your wealth of knowledge?" She raked her teeth against her throat. "Your wealth of experience?"

Thayer laughed with her and dropped her head back. "Does that mean you've finally accepted that I have no money?"

"Mmm, yes but…" Corey trailed kisses across her chest and over the tops of her breasts, displayed so beautifully in the bikini top. "You have many other wonderful riches to plunder."

Thayer pushed against Corey's shoulders to keep some distance between them. "Corey, stop. There are families here."

"I know." Corey was relentless in getting to her exposed skin of which there was plenty. "And I'm doing my best to normalize woman on woman love—for the children."

"You're ridiculous." Thayer sucked in a breath as Corey hit on a particularly sensitive spot. "And we're going to have to cut this walk short."

"It's a teaching moment."

Thayer successfully pushed her away, her eyes flashing mischievously. "If we head back now and your parents are still out, there may be time for me to teach you a lesson before dinner."

Corey grinned. "Yes, ma'am."

Thayer reached for Corey's hand again as they headed back down the beach the way they had come. "You know I've been thinking when we get back it may be nice to take a break from, um…" She trailed off.

"From what?"

"From *shenanigans*," Thayer finally finished.

"What?" Corey feigned shock. "That's no fun."

"Okay, how about we only entertain other people's drama and our lives remain blissfully uninspired."

"I'm sure you mean everywhere but in the bedroom, of course," Corey clarified.

"Of course."

"Then I wholeheartedly agree to undertake with you a life of unrelieved monotony."

They walked in silence for several minutes before Thayer added, "Only for a while."

"Just until the spring,"

"When the snow melts."

"Deal."